Falling Flat

Endorsements

Music, bugs, romance, and friendship, all wrapped in a fun camp package, makes for a great summertime or anytime read. Anyone who's ever been to camp will relate to Geri as she strives to fit in with new friends and frenemies, negotiates the trials of her first crush, and struggles to survive life in the woods. Love the clever music references woven throughout the narrative and dialogue.

—**Susan Miura**, award-winning author of the Healer series and *Signs in the Dark*.

Camp is bad enough—what with the creepy crawlies, suspect cafeteria food, and less-than-pleasant cabin arrangements. But dealing with camp drama, jealousy, interpersonal problems back home leaking into relationships, and sabotage ... Geri learns the power of reconciliation and new beginnings. The prose is rhythmically written, so much that you could swear it's actual music. And all the characters—flaws and all—have incredible depth. Teens will not only relate to this story, but yearn for more stories like this. I know when I was that age, I certainly did.

—**Hope Bolinger**, author of eighteen books, including the award-winning Blaze trilogy

I was swatting mosquitos and striving to be one of the cool kids at Camp Hi-Lu-Ma-Po while I read Carlson's debut novel Falling Flat. This hilarious—yet at times sobering—story shows the lives of young adults as they maneuver adolescence on their way to reaching for their dreams. I loved it!

—**Robin Luftig**, award-winning author and speaker, *Ladies of the Fire*

Falling Flat

Jenna Brooke Carlson

COPYRIGHT NOTICE

Falling Flat

Cover and Interior Design: Jeff Gifford, Derinda Babcock, Deb Haggerty

Editor(s): Julie B. Cosgrove, Deb Haggerty

PUBLISHED BY: Elk Lake Publishing, Inc., 35 Dogwood Drive, Plymouth, MA 02360, 2022

Library Cataloging Data

Names: Carlson, Jenna Brooke (Jenna Brooke Carlson)

Falling Flat / Jenna Brooke Carlson

224 p. 23cm × 15cm (9in × 6 in.)

ISBN-13: 978-1-64949-528-0 (paperback) | 978-1-64949-529-7 (trade paperback) | 978-1-64949-530-3 (e-book)

Key Words: Music, competition, romance, camp, ambition, bullies, friendship

Library of Congress Control Number: 2022935857 Fiction

DEDICATION

To Eve—who believed in me even when I didn't believe in myself

ACKNOWLEDGMENTS

This book wouldn't be possible without the incredible team at Elk Lake Publishing. Thank you, Cristel Phelps, for believing in this book. It means a lot that you saw something in Geri's story. Now others can share in her journey. Thank you, Julie B. Cosgrove and Deb Haggerty, for making my words and ideas sound polished. Your attention to detail is amazing, and I learned so much from you through the editing process. I'd also like to thank, Jeff Gifford and Derinda Babcock, for making the book look incredible, both inside and out. Because of your amazing designs, readers will be drawn to Geri's narrative and be able to enter into her world.

Next, I am extremely thankful to fellow writers who encouraged me in this process. I'd like to say thank you to my Page 7 Word Weavers critique group who hung in there through many chapter readings and offered valuable feedback. Robin, you've been there since the beginning—over seven years! Thank you for continuing to believe in Geri's story. Rosie, your love for Geri and Ethan holds a special place in my heart. Thank you for your enthusiasm, honest feedback, and encouragement.

I'm also grateful to my ACFW Chicago Chapter who helped me grow into the writer I am today. Chandra Blumberg, thank you for being a beta reader and giving valuable advice about the characters and their adventures. Susan Miura, thank you for offering your keen editorial expertise and continued support through the ups and downs of this journey. Candice Pedraza Yamnitz, your determination and creativity amaze me. Thank you for your consistent encouragement to pursue the publication of this book.

Additionally, I'd like to thank Rowena Kuo, who believed in a young girl with a bridesmaid tote bag and super rough draft. Thank you for seeing something in my manuscript from the very beginning. I'm also extremely grateful to Jessie Andersen, who gave me the feedback I needed to hear and the confidence to rewrite this novel. You told me publication was possible, and that hope has helped me continue to pursue this dream. Special thanks to Peggy Sue Wells, who gave me the encouragement I needed when I wanted to give up. Your reassurance that I had "it" strengthened me to keep going and write yet another draft of this story.

Many thanks to my family who has continued to support me in my writing dreams. My parents have always believed in me and stood by my side through thick and thin. I'd also like to thank my steadfast writing partner and beloved dog, Mia. Thank you for spending countless hours snuggling next to my computer. While you napped, I wrote and your tiny presence is such an encouragement to me. You offer me more comfort and support than you'll ever know.

Lastly, this book would not be possible without my Lord and Savior, Jesus Christ. God planted a love of reading into my very young heart. I grew up mesmerized by stories, and I hope to do the same for others. The themes in this book are based on God's grace and the firm foundation he's been in my life. I'm incredibly grateful for the favor he's shown to allow me to get my words out into the world.

CHAPTER 1

Trees. Lots and lots of trees. Trees meant bugs. Bugs bite. Bug bites meant nasty-smelling pink cream smeared all over me. I stepped out of the car, and my striped Keds touched the ground of the dreaded four-letter word—C-A-M-P.

Most kids probably love the campfires and sing-alongs and s'mores. OK, I won't complain about the s'mores, but with all the "Kumbaya" and bonding comes camp food. Besides, high ropes courses freak me out. So do cabins—and, well, cabins lead to bugs, bug bites, and oceans of calamine lotion.

Camp Hi-Lu-Ma-Po. The owners, Lucy and Maury Hipo concocted the bizarre name from their own names, which kinda matched the bizarre fact that I stood there.

The only reason I didn't hold on to the car-door handle for dear life? Camp Hi-Lu-Ma-Po claimed to be a performing arts camp. I needed its college scholarship. Armed with a piano, I could battle anything coming my way, even the bugs.

"Isn't this great, Geri?" My best friend, Abby, slid out of the back seat and opened her arms as wide as the line of pine trees in front of us.

"As great as the time your brother put a plastic spider in the shower." I crossed my arms.

My mom walked over to the passenger side of the car, her slight frame surveying the area around us. "You chose to come here. You could have stayed with your father while I—"

At the mention of his name, I became absorbed in the trees. Anything to avoid thinking of my cheating father. The tall pine trees mocked me, their green needles home to all types of horribly irritating insects. I took a deep breath, and the earthy smell of the woods filled my lungs. Gross. I exhaled the thoughts of my father along with the musty odor.

Mom walked around to face me. Her hazel eyes stared straight into my own. "Geri, were you listening to anything I said?"

I brushed back the wisps of mousy brown hair the annoying camp breeze had blown into my face. "No." I stood preoccupied sizing up my organic enemy. Nature.

Mom sighed. "It's camp for goodness sakes, not Death Valley." She popped the trunk. "Let's get the suitcases."

"C'mon Geri, stop being *dramatíca*." Abby fixed her long dark braid, the hair falling over the front of her tie-dye shirt. "We have two whole weeks together. Girl time diminishes sadness. Plus, I'm designating myself as your personal summer Spanish tutor. Mr. Iglesias won't know what hit him when you go back to class in the fall."

Her reasoning made sense. I couldn't be sad about spending time with my best friend. And I did need to get a better grade in Spanish. But did I have to do that all *here*? The annoying camp breeze displaced my hair again, but this time a gentle creak accompanied the woosh of the wind. It made me jolt.

"What's that?"

My left foot dipped into the edge where the road met the grass. I grabbed Abby's shoulder to keep from falling flat on my face. Wouldn't be a great way to start camp.

"*Cálmate*. I won't let the sign get you." Abby pointed toward an old wooden plaque swinging in the breeze. Its weathered letters read Camp Hi-Lu-Ma-Po: Perform to Shine.

The midday sun beat down on my face, and a flame lit in the pit of my stomach. I needed to shine to win the scholarship. I needed to shine brighter than anyone else there. I could suck it up for two weeks to win something life-changing. But I didn't have to be happy about the earthy escapade.

Mom set my suitcase on the asphalt, and I grabbed my flat-as-a-pancake pillow from the back seat. The comfort object easily squished into a ball if needed, perfect for any anxiety-ridden camp moments.

"Abby!"

Abby's braid whipped behind her back when she spun around. "Hey, Sarah!" She jogged to a girl in teal workout shorts. They embraced so hard I thought one of them might pop.

Mom's phone rang. She did the Dad eye roll. "Great, what does he want?" She stared at the screen while the tune played but finally answered.

"Yes, Stephen." She turned away from me. Didn't they know I could still hear them? Let me turn around and see if I get the magical power of teleportation.

"Of course we made it." Mom's voice sounded tense. "Do you think I'm incapable of driving her myself?"

Nope. Still in Flagstaff ... at camp.

They resembled dueling pianos, clashing out pounding notes. My parents had mastered a perfectly catastrophic composition. I folded the pillow over my ears and closed my eyes. Mozart. Beethoven. Bach. When I opened my eyes, I found myself looking at a—da capo—a repeat of what I'd just escaped.

Across the parking lot, a set of parent clones were in a yelling match, only the towering dad stood over the shorter

"Thanks." Abby took the plastic yellow bag from her, complete with a hint of the counselor's honeysuckle perfume.

"What's the other name?"

"Bruchi," I answered, "Geraldine Bruchi."

"Alrighty, Geraldine, you are in Cabin Twelve."

"Wait." I stepped closer. "There has to be a mistake. Check again. Abby and I signed up for the same cabin." I dropped my suitcase and bearhugged my pillow.

The counselor smacked her gum as she ran her finger down the list again. "Abigail Martínez, Cabin Eleven. Geraldine Bruchi, Cabin Twelve." She gave us a big smile and held my bag out to me. "Welcome to Camp Hi-Lu-Ma-Po!"

I turned to Abby. "Do something. You're the only good thing about this Hi-Ho-Dario place!"

Abby took my packet for me then smiled at the counselor. "Thanks for your help." She grabbed my arm and pulled me away from the registration table.

I hugged my pillow tighter. "We won't be spending tons of time together if we're not in the same cabin?"

"Calm down. I'm right next door. Plus, you'll meet people this way."

"I'm not here to *meet* people," I put my fingers up in air quotes around her words. "I'm here to win."

Abby planted her hands on her hips. "Is winning more important than relationships?"

Tears stung my eyes. "Relationships suck."

"Not all of them." She squeezed my arm. "Let's go to the Snack Shack after you get settled."

"Why?"

"To meet people that don't suck. *Está bien*. It's going to be OK, Geri. Promise."

Really? So far, camp appeared to be anything but OK.

Reasons I Don't Like Camp-

1. Bugs
2. Cabin assignment mix-ups

Reasons I Like Camp-

1. Abby

CHAPTER 2

I opened the cabin door like I would open Hayden's clavichord, hesitant and unsure what to expect. A musty odor filtered out the entryway. Log walls. Plank floors. Wooden ... everything. The only exception? White sheets and seafoam covers on the beds.

Bright beams of light shone on the walnut floor from windows on both sides of the door. Specks of dust danced in the sunshine. The cabin stood otherwise empty except for a spider moseying along the wooden floor. *Squish*. Intruder eliminated.

At least I got to choose which bunk I wanted. First to arrive gets first pick. Top bunk, hard to get in and out, ceiling overhead. Bottom bunk, easy to get into, closer to the spiders. Top bunk won. I threw my pillow up on the bed to the right.

A drop of sweat slid into my eye. Time for shorts. I flopped the suitcase on the bunk and rummaged through the contents. Deodorant, socks, toothbrush, T-shirts. I searched through the disheveled heap faster. Hairbrush, shoes, toothpaste, sheet music, scholarship essay.

Toiletries and clothing flew onto the wooden floor until I reached the bottom of the suitcase. No shorts. I hadn't brought any shorts!

"Welcome, Geri. What's your art of choice?" Julia rearranged her off-the-shoulder blouse.

"Piano. You?"

She put one hand on her hip and elongated her swan-like neck. "Ballet. I'm hoping to make it into NYU's intensive camp next summer. If we perform a classical piece this summer, I'll use the choreography for my audition."

Julia reached the top bunk bed across from mine in three long ladder strides then stripped the camp sheets from the mattress and threw them on the ground. She climbed back down to zip open her pink duffel bag. I had a feeling she had a constant to-do list running through her head, never stopping to take part in unproductive tasks.

Hannah clapped her hands together. "Then we're just waiting for Niki and—"

"Niki is in our cabin?" Julia froze in mid-air holding a ballet pink sheet set.

Hannah's smile grew an inch taller. "Yes, isn't that great?"

"As great as the time she overshadowed me in the production last year?"

"I know you didn't like losing, Julia, but a lot of the numbers required modern dance. You did great as a townsperson, and you earned a new experience. Isn't learning new things what camp's all about?"

Julia smoothed the new sheets on her mattress, but by smoothed I mean beat like a conga drum. "I want experience to help me become the best."

If you took out the lanky body, dancing experience, and everything pink, maybe this Julia girl and I had something in common.

"Maybe this year." Hannah turned toward me. "I'm crossing my fingers for you both."

"Hey, Hannah. You were my counselor last year. Hi, Julia." Abby's positive attitude burst through the door.

Hannah waved.

Julia raised her chin. I guess that qualified as a greeting in her mind.

"*Lista*, Geri? You ready?"

"To go home? Sure." I started down the ladder.

Abby rolled her eyes. "C'mon, let's go get something to eat." She turned toward the door then swiveled back around. "Wanna come, Julia?"

Julia leaped off her bed. "No, thank you. I'm going to run over to the dance studio. I missed my practice time this morning."

I followed Abby down the creaky steps and onto the gravel path. Huge pine trees lined the walkway. Their tall branches reached to the sky, shading us from the hot sun. Sunbeams speckled the ground, highlighting the daunting journey further into the camp.

"What's up with Julia?" I scurried to catch up with Abby's strides. "She's so ... intense."

Abby laughed. "She's determined, like you. She wants to dance for one of those big ballet companies in New York and knows she must be one of the best to get there. Do you know who else is in your cabin?"

I wiped my clammy forehead and secretly thanked Hannah for the shorts. "Hannah mentioned someone named Niki?"

"Oh no." Abby shook her head. "Those two together should be interesting."

"Why?"

"They're like fire and ice. Always fighting to be on top. I wish they'd realize there's room for both of them in the big dance world."

Abby might be right, but I understood Julia's perspective, too. Sometimes we *need* to be the best. Like when we need to escape our families and get to Juilliard.

We continued to walk down the dirt pathway where the trees grew denser and denser. A slight itch tickled my arm. I scratched at a non-existent bug. Others might not notice, but Abby knew me too well.

"*¿Qué pasa,* Geri?" Her eyes squinted.

"The bugs." I scratched faster.

Abby shook her head. "You're ridiculous. C'mon, we better hurry and get a snack if we're going to make it to the amphitheater in time for the camp welcome."

She sped up, but I let her go ahead of me. I'd been welcomed enough, thank you. If I wanted to sulk in the middle of nowhere Flagstaff, I had the right.

A creepy-crawly tickle brushed the back of my neck.

"No. No. No." I swatted myself and turned in circles while tugging at my shirt. "Get out! Abby! Help!" The pine trees spun faster and faster until I hit the grass, flat on my back.

A bright light of sequins practically blinded me. My vision cleared to see a pair of glaring blue eyes. The girl wore black shorts, a purple, sequined-tank top, and a long black cardigan. Who wears sweaters in July?

"You're lucky you didn't knock me over. I could have scuffed my new Jimmy Choo's." The curl of her ponytail fell to the side of her shoulder while she inspected her polka-dot wedges. Did she wear ridiculously expensive shoes to camp for a specific reason? Before I could say anything, she stomped off, her blonde hair bouncing as she walked.

Abby's pink sneakers appeared next to my head on the ground. "*¿Estás bien*, Geri?"

"If you call getting attacked by grouchy Miss Muffet and her evil spider *muy bien*."

Abby held out her hand. "Well, one is gone, and the other one ... don't let Chloe get to you."

I looked up at the tall trees and felt a bead of sweat trail down my forehead. It could have been worse, I guess. It could have been ten spiders. “I just lost my appetite.”

Abby sighed. “Then let’s head for the camp welcome.”

CHAPTER 3

A symphony of boisterous laughter and excited chatter filled the amphitheater. Rows of benches in a half-circle tilted down a slanted hill. Tall trees shaded the outskirts of the seats, giving the clearing an oh-so-happy camp feel for some, I guessed. For me, they spelled entrapment.

"Welcome, campers."

Maury's voice boomed from the camp stage. He stood in the center of an elevated rectangular wooden platform. The sun glistened off his balding head.

"Lucy and I are overjoyed to have you at Camp Hi-Lu-Ma-Po this year! We have two weeks of exciting things in store for you. Get ready for the best summer ever!" Maury raised his hands to the audience, encouraging cheers.

Abby shot me a told-you-so look.

Best summer ever? Not even close. How about the worst summer ever with the best possible outcome ... me walking home with a scholarship?

"As many of you already know, Camp Hi-Lu-Ma-Po takes pride in encouraging young people to pursue their passions, be creative, and develop their talents." Maury scanned his captive audience. "One way we do this is by having a Hi-Lu-Ma-Po performance every year. This year we've decided to add an extra challenge to help you develop an important and much-needed skill."

Abby raised an eyebrow at me.

My stomach lurched. I didn't need any extra challenges. I had enough already.

"To encourage teamwork in our ever-changing world, we will be requiring cabins to perform as their own teams this summer. You'll work with your teammates to create a number showcasing each other's strengths."

This couldn't be happening! First, Abby and I were separated. Now I couldn't perform with her. I'd never see her. My scholarship fate rested in the hands of strangers. No, not happening.

"Wait, wait, wait!" Someone shouted my objection. Good.

A sea of bewildered eyes turned to stare directly at me.

I whispered to Abby. "Did *I* say that out loud?"

"Yeah, you kinda did." Abby fidgeted on the bench.

My face felt as hot as the Phoenix sun on a mid-summer day.

"Is there a problem?" Maury shielded his eyes and scanned the crowd.

I looked to the pine trees for an escape, but they formed a secluded fence around this embarrassing moment. Instead, I became distracted by a set of piercing blue eyes two rows down. They belonged to the gorgeous boy with the ripped muscles.

I shook my head in slo-mo.

"Anyway ... " Maury continued with his announcements.

Abby bumped my leg. "You're acting ... weird."

My eyes remained glued to the back of the guy's head.

"Geri!" Abby hit my leg again.

"Ouch!" I looked at my annoying best friend.

"What are you looking at?" Abby looked in the direction of my eye-seared path.

"Nothing." I took one more peek at the mysterious guy.

Abby glanced his way. "If you are looking at Ethan, you better get in line." She nodded toward his bench. "And get a shield for Chloe's acrylic nails."

Ethan's maroon shirt strained against his broad shoulders. Then a blonde ponytail slid across his back, the end hanging in a perfect curl. Chloe, with the Jimmy Choos from the path, sat hip to hip with him.

I tapped Abby on the knee and pointed to Chloe. "Are they a thing?"

"Shhh!" A girl next to us spat out.

Abby shrugged and turned her attention back to Maury.

"It's time to head back to your cabins and get to know your team. I can't wait to see our talent show this year! Good luck, campers, and may the arts be with you!"

Maury finished with a chuckle, his round belly jiggling.

"Well, *chica*, we're competing against each other. Get excited or at least smile or something. This is going to be fun!" Abby shook my arms, I guess to transport her excitement into my body.

"I don't know the people in my cabin or if they're talented. For me to look good, we're all going to have to look good."

Abby squeezed my arm. "N*o te preocupes*. Don't worry. There are tons of talented people here. I'm sure you guys will create something amazing."

I sighed. "Maybe."

"Let's go, Ethan!" A shrill voice pierced my ears.

When I turned around, the reflection of a multitude of purple sequins blinded me. Chloe and Ethan strolled toward us.

Panicking, I ducked down behind Abby.

Abby looked at me behind her shoulder. "Real clever, Geri. There's no way they'll see you now."

"Shhh!" I grabbed Abby's calves. Like her petite legs would hide my ginormous panicking head. "They'll hear you."

"Ducking is not a talent, Newbie." Chloe huffed. "Actually, you should do a magical escape as your talent. Disappearing from the competition gives the rest of us more of a chance to shine."

Her cherry and vanilla perfume mixed with the forest air, the tainted and sour smell matching the perturbed look on her face.

"Come on, Chloe. Lighten up." Ethan knelt and held out his hand. His biceps glistened in the sunlight. Chisel-muscled sweating I didn't mind.

I stared at him like he had heroically saved me from getting stalled on a humongous roller coaster at Castles and Coasters. My brain tried to tell my fingers to take his hand, but my body froze. Brain cell malfunction.

Ethan smiled and the dimple on his left cheek formed. "I never did get your name, or should I call you Pillow Squisher?"

Speak self. Words aren't hard. My tongue stuck to the bottom of my mouth.

Abby nudged me with her heel, so I stood. What did he ask me again? Oh, my name. Geri. Two syllables.

"Well, Blurtatious Prototype? Or do you only speak when you're interrupting camp announcements?" Chloe glanced away as she wrinkled her nose.

I turned my eyes to the ground. The truth of her words stung. My leaded tongue remained anchored at the bottom of my clammy mouth.

"Knock it off, Chloe." Ethan's tone stiffened.

Ethan seemed awfully short with her. *Were* they a thing? Sitting and walking together insinuated dating.

Chloe pulled at the right sleeve of her black polka dot sweater. "She's frozen or something."

"Ethan, this is Geri." Abby came to the rescue. "And she does speak—" Abby put her hands on her hips. "—if people give her a chance."

She meant well, but I'm not sure her proclamation helped. I gave Ethan a quick smile. At least the corners of my mouth worked while my vocal cords remained broken.

"Everyone to their cabin." A counselor saved us from the awkward situation.

"Time to meet your cabinmates." Even meeting people sounded like a good exit strategy at the moment.

Chloe grabbed Ethan's hand. "Let's go, Ethan."

Hand holding also insinuated dating. Chloe pulled Ethan to the cabins and away from my beating heart. Why would a guy like that date a girl like her?

Ethan looked over his shoulder and waved. "Nice meeting you, Geri."

And there they went. The far-from-perfect girl with my perfect guy. And my tongue-tied action made me fall flat, again.

Reasons I Don't Like Camp–

3. *Chloe*
4. *Talent shows without Abby*
5. *Chloe with Ethan*

Reasons I Like Camp–

1. *Abby*

CHAPTER 4

Pranks, plants, pests, and gel pens. The annoyances summed up my prevailing camp experience.

I tapped the notecard in front of me with a sweaty pen in my hand. Like teambuilding didn't hold enough torture. We also had to melt in the sun.

Hannah sat across from me, her wavy brown hair now pulled up in a ponytail showing off her heart-shaped face. Julia posed to my left. Her blonde hair twisted up in a perfect knot on top of her head. She sat with her back as straight as mine during piano lessons, but instead of being mandated, hers seemed permanently fixed that way.

The only sound came from Niki, our newest cabin addition on my right. She clicked her tangerine pen in and out. "Let's get started." An intricate pattern of woven braids twirled across the top of Niki's head. She lifted the ponytail of braids from her neck. "It's too hot out here to wait around."

"We need everyone to begin." Hannah organized the pile of cards into a neat stack and sighed. "Why don't I go over the directions for the game while we wait?"

Sprayed down to ward off bugs. Lathered up and shielded from the sun's damaging rays. I now faced something else—teambuilding, honesty, and divulging information to strangers. How did I protect myself from this?

Great achievement is usually born of great sacrifice and is never the result of selfishness. Another great sacrifice right there.

"You need to write three things about yourself, but—"

High-pitched laughter interrupted Hannah. My heart took off for Destination Happiness when I spotted Ethan walking along the path. A second later, the bubbling bliss crashed into despair. Chloe stomped over my hopes in wedges taller than the treble clef's high C.

Hannah stood up. "Oh good, she's here."

My heart sped. You had to be kidding me. Cruella de Vil starred as our last cabin member. Fate pushed my dreams of winning the scholarship off a cliff. They were done. Dead. No more.

"Oh, great." Niki threw her pen on the grass. At least someone shared my feelings.

"Sorry to make you wait." Chloe flicked her manicured hand at Hannah. "Ethan wouldn't let me go." She put her white wide-rimmed sunglasses on top of her head and peered at me like she knew my innermost thoughts. Did she list mindreading along with manicuring and man-hoarding as one of her many talents?

"No worries." Hannah smiled. "Come have a seat."

"Yes, we have all day." Niki flashed a fake smile.

"I'm going to ignore that, Nicole." Chloe unwound herself from Ethan and moved toward us.

Niki rolled her eyes.

More fighting. The situation plunged from difficult to downright impossible. Maury's words echoed in my mind. *You'll work with your teammates to create a number showcasing each other's strengths.* What if we created a number showcasing the animosity everyone shows toward one another? The clash would be a showstopper.

"Let's make a spot for Chloe, girls." I felt bad for Hannah. Five minutes into her official camp counselor duties and our cabin screamed harmonic disaster.

"Hi, Chloe. Sit here." Julia scooched further to my left and made a space about half the size of Chloe. Not wanting to look like the rudest person on the camp planet, I moved to the right. The adjustment meant Sequin Queen would sit in between us, next to me.

"I'm going over the rules." Hannah handed Chloe a notecard and fuchsia pen. "You need to write three things about yourself, but only two are true. We'll have to guess which one is a lie."

1. *I can't stand having Chloe in my cabin.*
2. *I really can't stand having Chloe in my cabin.*
3. *I love having Chloe in my cabin.*

My blank notecard seemed to taunt me as I thought of something more reasonable to write. I wrote, "My parents are separated." I wished their split-up counted as the lie. Did covering the truth make the pain go away? I scratched the sentence out.

I glanced at the other girls, eyes fixed on the activity. Julia's bun pointed to the sky, her head titled over the paper. Niki fanned herself with a few spare notecards, jotting down ideas with the other hand.

I dare not look at Chloe. Those purple sequins blinded innocent bystanders, and I wanted to keep my vision, thanks. I turned back toward my card. Write something, self.

1. *I'm an only child.*
2. *I will go to Juilliard. Believing is the first step.*
3. *I come to camp every summer.*

"Everyone ready?" Hannah replaced the question with a wide smile. "I'll go first."

Within a few minutes, we had learned Hannah studied dance at Arizona State University, Niki had two brothers, and Julia spent an hour a day walking around her house in pointe shoes to develop her arch.

Chloe went next. She read, "I love dogs." Clearly a lie since she resembled Cruella De Vil. "My favorite color is pink." Believable. "We got our swimming pool cabaña remodeled two summers ago." Did she have an ad for a mansion going up soon?

"I think purple is your favorite color since you're wearing a violet top." Julia pointed to Chloe's shirt. "Number two is the lie."

Chloe straightened her back to sit tall. "Both suit me, but pink is my favorite."

Hannah pointed her pen at Chloe. "I think the first one is a lie. You seem more like a cat person to me."

I agreed with Hannah. If Chloe had a dog she would have to give it toys, baths, walks ... walking a dog in wedges. Watch out. Cruella overboard.

Niki sighed. "The last one is the lie. I know you were living with a different fam—"

"You're not supposed to guess if you already know, Nicole." Chloe pointed her pen at her.

I allowed myself to look at Chloe now. Seeing her divulge secrets trumped the eye risk. I thought I saw wetness around the outside of her eyes, but the glistening could have been sweat from wearing long sleeves in ninety-degree heat.

"Then why did you say anything about where you live?" Niki leaned to gaze at her.

"Because ..." Chloe slid the sunglasses from the top of her head to her nose. "We're getting the cabaña remodeled this summer. The project should be close to finished when

I get back home. The pool's going to have the cutest wet bar with mosaic tiles."

Niki inspected her tiger orange nails. "We get it. Your new folks are rich. La-de-da-de-da. Ever since you moved in with them you've acted like you're better than the rest of us. News flash. You're not."

Chloe shot up like Old Faithful in heels. "Well, I never." Her face grew bright red, and I swore I saw steam coming out of her ears. I hoped this didn't happen every hour and a half like in Yellowstone.

Hannah stood up and put her hand on Chloe's shoulder. "Girls." She looked back and forth between her and Niki. "I'm sure no one meant to—"

Chloe pointed a talon at Niki. "She said those things on purpose. She always has these side comments. I don't need to stay here and take this."

She stomped off toward the front of the cabin leaving me and my notecard unconfessed. Maybe my secrets wanted to stay hidden. Chloe's clearly did. I guess we had one thing in common.

Reasons I Don't Like Camp–

6. ***Chloe in my cabin***

Reasons I Like Camp–

1. ***Abby***

CHAPTER 5

Some people make Mac 'n Cheese with the right cheese and noodle consistency. Some make the dish like noodle and cheese soup. Camp chose the soup option.

"I can't believe Ethan let the Queen Bee strike him with her venom once again." Niki thunked her hand on the light oak table.

"Again?" I looked out the bright sunny windows lining the back of the cafeteria, trying to envision Ethan with the Chloe monster. Their relationship didn't make sense.

"They were going out last summer but broke up at the end of camp." Abby shoveled another scoop of macaroni into her mouth, the soupy sauce dripping from the edge of her spork. "Looks like they might be back together."

"Boys are too much of a distraction." Julia sat pin straight. The Mac 'n Cheese should have ordered an elevator to her mouth.

"A welcome distraction." Niki lifted her eyebrows and wiggled them.

Julia shook her head and concentrated on her lunch. The veggie to carb ratio on her plate was 3:1. Either she ate like a health nut or couldn't stand the sad excuse for macaroni.

I turned to Niki. "Do you have a boyfriend back home?"

"Eh, boys." She swatted the air. "Who needs 'em."

"Niki's too busy anyway." Abby shrugged.

"With hip-hop?" I couldn't see how.

Niki turned back to her plate. "Yeah, I spend afternoons at the studio, but I also help my mom out with my sisters, and I'm juggling a lot of stuff at school. I need to keep up my GPA to get into a good college and hopefully go to law school someday."

"Wow, that's amazing." I forced a smile, but my stomach dropped. Law school. Lawyer. Divorce.

I found a business card next to a Cheerio on the kitchen floor last week. I had picked the paper up expecting one of those landscaper advertisements you get in the mail, but the words read much different. David E. Cohen. Family Law. Even though I stayed mad at my dad, I had hoped my mom meant to throw the card away like a yard maintenance ad. Divorce blared final.

I pushed the noodle boats around my plate. Oops, cheese water overboard.

"*Bueno*, Geri." Abby grabbed a napkin to dry up the yellow puddle. "You need a major intervention. I'm not going to let you ruin your summer."

Abby knew me too well. I needed another gloomy day as much as I needed to forget another pair of shorts.

I captured a noodle vessel with my plastic utensil. "What do I need to do?"

Abby's café eyes bubbled. "I'm glad you asked. First things first: Your piece for the Hi-Lu-Ma-Po talent show!"

"Did you forget we aren't working together?" I widened my eyes. Duh.

"No, I didn't forget, but a true friend encourages no matter what." She banged the end of her silverware on the table.

"You may be a true friend, but I'm a true competitor." Niki threw her shoulders back.

"I agree with her on this one," Julia pointed her spork at me.

Wow. She agreed with Niki. Would a pig fly through the cafeteria next?

"We are performing to shine above all the other pieces." Julia crunched on a baby carrot.

"If outdoing the rest of us is going to cheer up Grumpy over here, please do," Abby pressed her hands together.

Maybe a quick prayer?

"Uh-hum, who are you calling Grumpy?" I threatened Abby with a spork of soupy Mac 'n Cheese.

"You wouldn't." Abby squinted.

I put my finger on the end of the spork.

"Geraldine ..."

"Just for that—" I pulled my finger back and let the noodles fly.

Abby ducked. The macaroni hit a redheaded boy's neck behind her. He turned, took a handful of carrots, and threw them in my direction. His aim, however, proved to be worse than mine and the orange explosion blew up on a carton of milk next to me. The milk poured into its owner's lap. She reacted by hurling the carton at the person across from her, and before I could say "Piano Sonata 126", the whole cafeteria erupted in a wild uproar. Food flew faster than Beethoven's fingers and the noise level *crescendoed* at an *allegro* pace. In a matter of seconds, I had salad dressing in my hair, Mac 'n Cheese all over my face, and milk dripping from my ear.

A high-pitched whistle screeched, and the flying food dropped to the floor. The frenzy halted after an olive hit me in the nose. "All right, all right." Marty's voice loomed. "Who started this?" A glop of noodles dropped on Marty's head from the wooden beams lacing the ceiling.

The redheaded victim of the first spoonful of Mac 'n Cheese pointed to me. Maury walked over. "Miss ..."

"Geri Bruchi." I shook my head trying to get the dripping milk to stop tickling my ear.

"Miss Bruchi, is throwing food appropriate cafeteria behavior?" He walked closer to me, along with his red squished face.

"It was an accident, Mr. Hipo." I held up my hands, and cheesy noodles plopped onto the floor, which didn't help my case.

Mr. Hipo eyed the gloppy starch. "And how did you *accidentally* throw food at another camper?"

"I didn't accidentally throw macaroni. I meant to throw food at her." I pointed at Abby who still held a handful of red Jell-O cubes.

"Oh, Miss Martìnez also started this?" Maury turned to face Abby.

"No, Mr. Hipo. Abby had nothing to do with the mix-up." I grabbed a napkin and wiped the evidence off my hands.

"Then I guess *you* will be cleaning the mess. Campers, the show is over. Please return to your cabins." Mr. Hipo stomped off toward a room in the back of the cafeteria.

Mumbling campers exited, each glaring in my direction.

And once again, I felt as if I'd fallen flat on my face.

"*No te preocupes*, Geri," Abby dropped the Jell-O out of her hand and shook lettuce out of her hair. "We'll help."

"Yeah, Geri. A food fight is a pretty cool stunt to play on your first day." Niki appeared next to Abby, picking shredded cheese off her shirt.

"Mr. Hipo!" Abby called. "Two more mops!"

Maury wheeled a mop and yellow bucket out of the closet. "I'll need help wheeling them out then."

"Coming, Mr. Hipo." Abby brushed more food from her leg.

"You guys don't have to do this, honest." I felt even more embarrassed now.

"Niki?" Abby swiveled in her direction as she scooped up some more jello. "Did you have fun?"

"When is it not fun to have salad dressing up your nose?"

"See." Abby winked, then jogged over to the broom closet.

Niki and I burst out laughing.

"I'm glad you're going to enjoy this." Maury handed me a mop and yellow bucket before putting a pile of rags on a nearby table. "Make sure this place looks good as new."

"Yes, sir." I lowered my eyes to a plop of salad dressing near my shoe.

"And Geri?"

"Yes, Mr. Hipo?"

"You have a crouton in your hair."

Maury walked out chuckling. I brushed the top of my head, and the salad topping fell to the floor with all the other scattered food. Good thing I had reinforcements to clean the place up.

Abby returned with two other sets of mops and buckets, and we took different sides of the room. I decided to head over to the entryway where the sunlight streamed from a row of windows onto the messy floor. Then I'd be cleaning on sunshine.

A puddle of juice pooled near the front door. The orange liquid stretched from the entry to a nearby table and chair. I dipped the mop in the bucket of soapy water before wringing the end out in the top container.

A few seconds later, the screen door squeaked open. I met those sparkling blue eyes, and my stomach flopped like the yarn strands in the soapy bucket. Ethan tousled his caramel brown hair and smiled.

"Need help?"

Great. Pillow face, muted vocal cords, crusty food. I nailed first impressions. Without waiting for me to answer, which could have taken a hundred years, Ethan grabbed a rag and wiped a nearby table. I moved the mop to the puddle, even though my mouth felt numb.

"You were responsible for this?" Ethan glanced in my direction.

"Uh-huh." At least I managed to mutter an answer.

"Geri, right?"

I nodded and took a deep breath. Beethoven. Haydn. Grieg.

I could have used reinforcements but Abby and Niki worked in the far corners of the cafeteria.

"Do you normally mute out the world, or is pillow-squishing a new camp ritual?"

"My parents ..." I'm not sure if I stopped because I realized I actually spoke audible words to Ethan or because I didn't want to let my secret out, not yet.

"No need to explain." He gave me a half-smile.

The red faces of Ethan's parents came to mind. "The fighting burns my ears." The words lifted from my tongue and plopped onto the ground with orange juice. It felt good to have the mess out on the laminate floor instead of smashed into my body.

"How long have yours been at it?" Ethan brushed tomatoes and cheddar cheese from the table into his hand.

"A few months. How about yours?" I swished the mop back and forth to absorb the puddle. The tendrils danced along the edges of the tangerine pool, taking the liquid with them.

"Since my dad figured out my mom cheated on him." Ethan looked out the windows near the door. His eyes seemed to hold the weight of a baby grand.

I didn't know what to say. I couldn't imagine spilling secrets to someone I just met.

Ethan shook his head and went back to cleaning, the rag squeaking against the already clean table. "The only time they quit is when we get out of the car for church on Sunday—until the moment they get back in after service is over." He rolled his eyes. "God knows they fight, even if they manage to be quiet for an hour and a half in his house."

"Yeah." I moved the heavy mop back to the bucket unsure of how to talk to a cute honest stranger. "Me too."

"Oh, yeah? Where do you go?"

"Not the church part, but the covering up part." I pulled the black handle to wring out the orange juice. The yellowy liquid flowed from the top container into the large water basin below.

I decided to focus on a huge puddle of milk further down the way while Ethan moved closer to the door. He scrubbed at a table with enough force to put a hole through the wood. For a moment we worked in silence, my mind crowded with thoughts and tape-recorded arguments. Maybe his, too.

I managed to get the milk but needed to squeeze the mop in a bucket next to the door. Next to Ethan. I froze for a second, biting my bottom lip. The liquid trickled back on the floor.

"Here let me help you." Before you could say "Wolfgang Amadeus Mozart," Ethan stood in front of me with the bucket. My gaze remained pinned on his steel-blue eyes, but I managed to thank him.

"Are you excited about the talent show?" Ethan either tried to make conversation or wanted to break the awkwardness of my staring.

"I'm excited to win." I dropped the mop in the wringer.

"And you're modest too." Ethan smiled.

"I'm determined." I pulled the handle to squeeze out the mop. "I need to win the college scholarship to go to Juilliard."

"What do you play?"

"Piano. You?" Dumb question since he had a guitar strapped to those awesome back muscles when we first locked eyes.

"Guitar." He sighed. "I have big dreams too. I'm hoping God has the same plan."

I envisioned God in heaven with my life plan in his hands. He scribbled the details on a memo pad. If God had plans for me, they couldn't involve me living in a parental war zone. Could they?

I wrung out the already dry mop a few more times, deciding how to respond.

Ethan found audible words first. "You want to practice tomorrow?"

I bounced the handle between my hands. "Maybe, if you're not busy with Cruella." I stopped and bit my lip. I honestly didn't mean to reply out loud.

"What?"

My mouth filter had come off. My fingers froze and the mop plummeted to the floor. The handle crashed on the linoleum, and I scrambled to pick up my mess. "You seemed to be pretty busy earlier with someone. Chloe, maybe? If you're not busy and I'm not busy ..." When I stood up, I knocked over the bucket and murky water rushed over the floor splashing my shorts.

Ethan grabbed the edge of the bucket and lifted the mop from the floor. I bent down to help even though I remained useless unless my hands magically transformed into absorbent material.

"Tough day, huh?" Ethan cleaned the spill.

"Yeah." I sat on the damp floor. "Sorry about the water."

"Don't worry about it." He put the mop in the bucket. "Would you say your day couldn't get any worse?"

I put my chin on my hands. "I'm sure the universe could find a way."

Ethan reached his hand out to me. "Let me try to battle the universe on this one then."

"What are you thinking?" I took Ethan's hand, and he pulled me to my feet. The warmth of his touch radiated to my twirling heart.

"A jam session. Tomorrow."

I looked from Ethan to the rag floating in the gray water toward me as I sat in Hannah's soggy shorts.

"Sure, why not?"

CHAPTER 6

The amphitheater filled with the droning sound of crickets and lively chitchat. Abby had convinced me to lie on a blanket in the grass near the projection screen. While we weren't the only ones on the ground, why someone would voluntarily make themselves mosquito bait was beyond me.

Julia stretched out in front of us, her tall frame taking up the length of the blanket while she chatted in Polish on her phone. A tight bun poked out from a travel pillow nestled underneath her head. The girl thought of everything.

"You have to tell me the whole story." Abby spread her arms to the twinkling sky above. "It's your first day at camp, and you're already giving Chloe a run for her hunny. You're bold, Geri, super bold."

"I am not." I grabbed the bug spray and doused myself in the repellent. Never can be too careful. With bugs or men.

The smell of eucalyptus spread out around us. Abby turned on her side to face me. She coughed and swatted at the mist disappearing into the air. Insect repellent would not deter her from the subject at hand. "Maybe not willingly, but when she finds out he asked you out ..."

I collapsed on the fleece blanket and looked at the stars. "He did not. He offered to practice. I practice with my piano teacher, and he's the Grinch pre-Cindy Lou Who. You don't see me calling my lessons a date."

"But the Grinch doesn't have dreamy hair and dreamy eyes." Abby turned back toward the sky. "At least now we know they're not a thing."

A couple sat on a plaid blanket to our right. The guy had his arm draped over the girl's tanned shoulder and she held his large hand in her fingertips. He whispered something in her ear, and she titled her head back as she laughed. For all I knew, Chloe and Ethan mirrored a similar scene somewhere in the vast dark wilderness.

I sighed. "We don't know that."

"If he asked you out, he's not dating her."

"We've already been through this." I put my hands under my head. "When is this movie starting?"

"You're changing the subject."

"Maybe, but this movie needs to get going, or I'm going to become the Grinch myself sitting in this insect bait zone for no reason." I scratched my arms. "The mosquitos are horrible."

"Julia doesn't seem to mind." Abby pointed in the direction of my relaxing teammate. "Plus, you have enough bug spray to ward off a small army. I haven't seen one."

"Really? I see two pests right now." A screechy voice hovered above us.

We jerked upright to see Chloe impeding on our space.

"*Hablando del rey de roma*." Abby whispered. "Speaking of ..."

Chloe wasn't alone. Three tall, skinny, blonde, Chloe clones stood next to their majesty. All four of them had high ponytails, with hair pinned around the elastic, like they were telling the ponytail, "We aren't ordinary people here who wear ordinary, everyday ponytails. We're too special."

"And I see three with you." Niki's attitude joined us right in time.

The girls didn't look like they intended to acknowledge Niki's comment at all. One popped her gum while staring at the sky, another inspected her acrylic French manicure, and the last one's eyes looked at us like we were day-old ravioli beginning to crust at the bottom of a buffet bar.

"I'm sorry. Is there someone speaking here?" Chloe looked right over Niki's head into the darkness.

"On the phone here," Julia shouted without turning around.

Everyone ignored her. I looked at Abby, and she shrugged.

"What do you got there?" Niki pointed to a bright pink tote bag hanging on Chloe's shoulder.

Chloe adjusted the handle on her arm. "Movie night necessities."

"Like what? A battery-operated curling iron in case your hair goes flat?" Niki grinned.

Chloe rolled her eyes. "If you recall, I'm not talking to you, Nicole."

Abby patted a spot next to us. "Niki, do you want to sit—"

"I don't know why you got all bent outta shape when I was just speaking the truth." Niki cut her off.

I gotta hand it to Abby for trying to create a diversion, but Niki and Chloe had argumentative tunnel vision. Reminded me of two parents I knew ...

Chloe's hands formed two fists at her side. "The truth! How about—"

"Oh, girls, I'm glad we found you." Hannah's cheerful smile interrupted the daylong feud ... year-long feud ... lifelong feud? I couldn't tell if Hannah ignored the fight on purpose or remained oblivious to the whole thing. My gut told me she chose to overlook the argument.

"*Do usłyszenia.*" Julia ended her call and sat up. "Hannah, we're happy you're here." Julia breathed a deep sigh and turned around. Her tight face told me she didn't have patience for unnecessary drama.

"Are we all sitting here? I brought another blanket." Hannah lifted a star quilt.

"I'm not staying with certain company." Chloe jolted her head to the side, the edge of her ponytail following the motion.

"Oh, c'mon girls. Movie night is a relaxing time for cabins to spend together." Hannah spread her blanket next to Abby's. "Let's start over, get to know one another. We all have positivity inside of us." Hannah motioned to Chloe's bag. "Oh good, Chloe. Did you bring movie snacks?"

"Not exactly." Chloe shifted her weight.

Hannah narrowed her gaze at a spot out in the darkness. "I need to talk to a friend real quick, but make yourselves comfortable. I'll be right back. Remember, this is going to be a great time to get to know each other better."

"She's right. This is cabin bonding time. I need to go find mine, but you girls borrow the blanket." Abby squeezed my shoulder before standing up. "I'll catch up with you tomorrow. Remember. Positivity."

I *was* positive—positive our cabin would never be able to work together.

"Fine by me." Niki lay down on Abby's blanket. "I could go for relaxing. This day has been too much."

"Not fine with me." Chloe crossed her arms. In response, Bubble Gum blew another bubble, Nails fixed her hair with her talons, and Eyes continued to stare ready to devour us, even if we were crusty old food.

Julia breathed an audible sigh and stood. "Niki. Geri. Stand up."

Her tone reminded me of my mother's when I got in trouble.

"Chloe." Julia folded her arms.

Her Majesty turned around. I guess Julia hadn't done anything to offend her yet, or maybe they bonded by being the blonde domineering type.

"Here's how I see things. We're all together in this cabin so we have to perform together. We need to put the hostility aside to have a decent number for the talent show."

"I guess I care more about the performance than *her*." Chloe nodded toward Niki.

"So, we agree on something." Niki faked being surprised with a dramatic hand slap to her cheek.

"Good. Now let's get on with our evening." Julia sat on Hannah's quilt with her perfect balletic posture.

"Are they staying for our bonding session?" Niki pointed to the three Chloe clones.

"We should get to our cabins too." Bubble Gum blew a small blush-colored balloon before engulfing the stickiness with a loud smack.

"All right, see ya later." Niki waved her hand like she was warding off a pesky fly and stepped back on the quilt.

Hannah returned. "Everyone's still here. Did we figure the situation out?"

Niki stretched out on the blanket. "No drama here."

"Great." Hannah smiled. "Let's all get settled then."

I took a seat next to Niki, and Hannah sat by Julia. Finally, movie time. Something I could handle. Maybe camp life wouldn't be completely intolerable. The air felt cooler at night ...

My heart stopped as the deafening sound of a vacuum broke any amount of peacefulness.

Niki jolted up and turned around. "You've got to be kidding me."

Right behind our blankets, Chloe held a nozzle to a blow-up chaise lounge. The pink plastic rose about an inch off the grass and grew with every second of air pump insanity. Every camper within a mile radius stared at Chloe and her ridiculous camp furniture.

"I thought you said no drama, Nicole." Julia clucked her tongue.

Niki put her hands up and turned to me. "If she wants to be the princess, so be it. Should we get a pea to test her validity?"

I giggled before turning back to the projector. The movie's drum roll tune played in my head trying to block out Chloe's blaring blow-up lounger. The air pump shut off in time for the last few bars played by the trumpets.

"Good enough." Chloe sat behind us as her lounger protested with crinkles and creaks.

"I'm surprised anything is good enough for the princess," Niki whispered.

"Excuse me?" Chloe leaned forward and her pink plastic squeaked.

Niki stuck two thumbs in the air. "Enjoy the show."

"Everyone ready?" Hannah eyed each of us. "The movie's starting."

Ready for what? A movie? Sure. Our combustible camp crew? Not so sure.

CHAPTER 7

Trying to fuse our cabin would be easier than making ground beef inside a chocolate cake taste scrumptious. Wait, that might be for dinner tonight.

The mid-morning sun beat down as we embarked on our first talent show practice, or as Hannah called the huddle, "a brainstorming session." My sweat glands revved to overdrive in the Arizona heat, and my nerves raced when I thought about Cabin Twelve holding my fate in their hands.

I wished I could melt right into the grass, away from camp and any unyielding expectations of myself, but then I couldn't win the scholarship. Instead, I sat up and tried to be an active participant. We needed to figure this out for Juilliard's sake.

"Our piece should be ballet-focused." Julia put her arms up in a perfect balletic circle above her head. "Ballet is timeless. The audience will love a classical piece." She pointed her toes in a wide "V" while sitting on the grass.

"More like classically boring," Niki flopped her legs on the ground in front of her. "How about a more modern piece? I know you love ballet, Julia, but Swan Lake isn't my main forte if you know what I mean."

Julia lowered her arms to a perfect "T", extending her fingers to the edges of the yard before leaning over and stretching to the left side. "You got to dance your style last summer. Plus, ballet dates back to the 1500s. We'd be part of carrying on the tradition."

Hannah sat in the middle, glancing between Julia and Niki. Then, she starred at the sky. Did she seek inspiration? Say a prayer? Hope a UFO would zap her up?

I didn't know what direction to go, but we needed to embed piano in our piece. A ballet number would allow me to play a classical composition. I hadn't ventured as much into more "modern" music, but I wanted Niki to be happy too.

Chloe slid the white sunglasses on top of her head to the bridge of her nose. "We should lead the piece with vocals and have the dance floating in the background."

Niki cocked her head to the side and her braids cascaded over her shoulder. "Yes, I'm sure you would love being front and center, pushing the rest of us to the side like you did last year when you—"

"You want to have a great performance, don't you?" Chloe graced her neck with her acrylic nails. "My voice ensures success."

Niki's back grew an inch taller, and she placed her hands on her knees. "How about the dancing is front and center and the vocals *float* in the background?"

"Yes, the ballet." Julia folded her arms over her chest.

I should drop the piano on all of them and call the move artistic expression. My head ached, so I rubbed my temple with my finger. Agreeing on a piece for the talent show seemed like musician impossible.

"Girls, I know we all have unique talents we want to showcase, but we need to blend our skills to make everyone happy." Hannah put her hands together and leaned her chin on them.

"She'll only be happy if she's front and center." Niki pointed at Chloe.

"Let's try it." Hannah stood.

"I'm sorry. What?" Niki stood and brushed the dirt off her athletic shorts.

"I'm not saying we have to go with this formation but we need to try something. Maybe moving will get the creative juices flowing." Hannah motioned for the rest of us to stand.

"I'm not opposed." Chloe rose on her blush pink wedges.

"And what ballet and hip-hop song do you sing?" Niki crossed her arms.

"Do you only dance hip-hop, Niki?" Julia raised her long legs on the ball of her foot.

"No."

"Do you dance ballet?"

"I started with Cecchetti, but—"

"Let's try a classical piece then. For the creative juices." Julia pulled her toe to the side, reaching her head.

"I know fantastic operatic pieces. Ballet would complement the songs and my voice." Chloe leaned back on her right hip.

Niki shook her head. "I'm sorry. *What?*"

Hannah bent down next to her. "Let's at least try."

Niki's mouth formed a tight line across her face. "All right." She tucked her red Camp Hi-Lu-Ma-Po tank top into her waistband. The color of her shirt matched the stripe on her light gray shorts. "But as soon as I find a better idea, we're doing whatever that is."

"Thank you." Hannah sighed and turned to me. "And Geri, can we say you'll play Chloe's music? I know this is all a stretch. We're just trying something."

"Sure." And then afterward why don't I give the Queen a pedicure, maybe get her an ice-cold lemonade with a bright pink umbrella? Insert dramatic eye roll.

Hannah put her hands on Niki and Julia's shoulders. "Let's get changed and head over to the dance studio. Geri and Chloe, I know you won't be dancing, but we should all stay together and support the team."

Team? There's supposed to be no "I" in team. This cabin would be the iTeam.

I rubbed the back of my clammy neck. The base of my hair felt damp with sweat. I peered at the sun, trying to will its warmth behind a cloud.

Hannah patted my back. "The studio's air-conditioned."

I looked at her. "Sure." I wish I could say I wanted to be a team player, but the promise of a cooler space spoke to me. If we were going to argue, I'd rather fight without melting.

"I'll oversee the music selection and make sure the melody suits my voice." Chloe lowered her shades and peered through the top of the lens.

Niki headed toward the cabin. "This isn't a for sure thing," she called over her shoulder.

Hannah motioned to the rest of us. "C'mon girls. We leave for the studio in ten."

Poor Hannah. She tried to pull us together, but we failed her.

Once inside, Chloe made a beeline for her bed. She plopped on the covers and thumbed through her phone, twitching her right wedge-clad foot. The thick sole contrasted her thin legs. Weighted footwear had to build up ankle strength.

Julia pulled a leotard and a pair of knit shorts from her bag. She tucked the duffle under Niki's bunk before draping the one piece over her shoulder. Her shoulders jutted back as she headed to the bathroom. Julia missed no opportunity to present her perfect posture.

Since I didn't need to change, maybe I'd call my mom. I hadn't talked to her since I'd left, and she sat at home all alone. I reached for my phone on top of my bed and tucked the cell in my pocket.

"Hey, Geri?"

I turned to see Niki scrounging at the bottom of her suitcase. "Yeah?"

She nodded toward me. "Are those your favorite shorts?"

My cheeks grew warm. "Oh, these are Hannah's." I looked at our counselor scribbling in a journal. "I forgot to pack any."

Niki revealed three pairs of cotton ones from behind her back. "I figured. Here, take these. They're elastic so they should fit all right."

I looked into her warm caramel eyes. "Thanks, Niki. That means a lot." Now I could at least rotate my borrowed clothing collection.

"No problem." She turned back to her bag and pulled out a pair of black spandex shorts. "Plus, I'll be living in these with all the dancing anyway."

I finished slipping them into my suitcase when Julia appeared from the bathroom. She bent over to grab something from her bag, revealing several zig-zag straps along the back of the black leotard. A pair of ballet flats dropped on the floor without much of a sound followed by the thud of her toe shoes. After tucking both pairs in a tote bag, she slid a swing dress over her leotard.

Julia smoothed the sides of her sleek hair. "Ready people?"

Niki held up a pair of black sneakers. "Ready as I'll ever be."

"You're going to dance ballet in those?" Julia's mouth twisted as she pointed at the shoes.

Niki shrugged. "Sneakers are all I've got. I only pack my ballet shoes when I have to, a.k.a. the one class I take a week."

Julia dropped her tote to the floor. "No problem. I've got an extra pair."

Of course she did. I wouldn't be surprised if she had a leotard for each day of the week.

"I'm not putting my feet in your stinky shoes."

Julia's eyes narrowed. "What are you—"

Niki put her hand up. "I'm not declining because of you. I know what shoes smell like after practicing. I wouldn't wear anybody's, even Hannah's. No offense, Hannah."

Hannah closed her journal. "None taken. And I don't blame you. Bring the jazz shoes. They'll be fine for starting with ideas."

Niki nodded. "Great."

"Ready, Chloe?" Hannah raised her voice a tad.

Chloe thudded her wedges on the wooden floor. "Yup. I created a playlist of songs to showcase my vocals." She dropped her phone in a bow-adorned purse and threw the bag over her shoulder.

Niki opened her mouth, shook her head, and remained silent. Thank goodness for her self-control. If everyone could get along better, maybe we'd have a shot. My eyes tick-tocked between Niki's slight frown and Julia's glowing smile. Finding harmony seemed like a *long* shot.

CHAPTER 8

The birds' melodies helped cover our cabin's hovering awkwardness. The Fantastic Four and their fearless leader marched on to fight the evil villain of camp-enforced team bonding. Could I be the Invisible Woman, please?

Down the path, we reached a protruding sign with carved directions. An arrow pointed to the dance studio on the left. Underneath the label, an opposite symbol directed campers to the music studio. Now I needed the superpower of cloning so I could practice instead of joining the Drastic Four.

Hannah pointed to the left. "This way, girls."

I left any hope of multiplying and followed the girls in the direction of the dance studio. A large wooden building came into view. Above the door hung a white weathered sign with the camp's name and motto.

A blast of cool air hit my face when I stepped inside. Plexiglas windows decorated the long hallway. The room smelled like a strange mix of perspiration and cotton as if someone had attempted to use an air freshener, but the poor thing didn't stand a chance next to dancers' sweat.

"This is what I'm talking about," Niki stood right in front of the vent. "I'd dance ballet in exchange for this air conditioning."

Chloe rubbed her arms. For the first time, wearing a long-sleeved sweater made sense.

Hannah peeked into the first room on the right. "Hey, Sam, any rooms open?"

A counselor with long black hair to her waist stepped out into the hall. "Hey, girls. Yeah, Studio Two is open."

Hannah smiled. "Thanks. This way, girls."

We walked down the worn-carpeted hall to the second room on the left. Light oak planks lined the floors, and a showcase of mirrors outlined the room. Two long beams hung along the opposite walls.

Julia slipped on her ballet shoes and darted to a barre. "Let's warm up, girls."

By girls, she meant Niki.

Niki slipped her sneakers on at a snail's pace and headed to the middle of the floor. She placed her hands on her thighs landing in a deep squat. She stretched one hand over her head and then the other.

Chloe pounded over to the speakers, her white shorts swaying side to side. A long cable trailed onto the floor. Chloe plugged in her cell and turned a knob on the stereo. She tapped her phone and a familiar R&B tune filled the room.

"Absolutely not. Needs to be more classical." Julia bent her right leg while her other toe stretched to the top barre.

Niki twirled in a few circles across the floor. "This music could work. The song has a lyrical vibe ... the style would be a good compromise."

Julia dropped her left leg back to the ground. "We said we would try ballet. Right, Hannah?"

Hannah sighed and put her hand on my shoulder. "Geri, we've got a few things to figure out, and I know you don't have a job right now. Feel free to take five."

A break sounded perfect, and I could call my mom. Plus, I didn't want to watch the impending dance catastrophe. The disaster would remind me of how far I stood not only from winning the scholarship but having a chance at the money altogether.

Hannah walked toward Chloe and the stereo. "I'll pick the song."

Chloe held her phone closer. "But—"

"We're trying things, remember? I promise when we decide on something, you'll have a say in the song." Hannah narrowed her gaze.

Time for me to go. I'd been around enough fighting lately. Maybe I'd take ten.

I walked into the hall and took my phone out of my pocket. The screen revealed two missed calls. Mom and my deplorable father. My stomach churned at the sight of his name. Leave me alone, Stephen. You did too much to get a callback.

One bar of service showed on the screen. I walked back to the front of the dance studio and another bar appeared. I pressed on Mom's name. The line rang twice before she picked up.

"Hi, honey. How's it going?" Her comforting tone warmed my heart.

Through the Plexiglas, Julia stood with her arms folded talking to Niki.

"It's going."

"Doesn't sound too positive." Mom said.

I took a big breath. "The experience isn't positive. I'm separated from Abby. I have to work with the cabin from the Black Lagoon. This is ruining my chances for the scholarship." I leaned my head against the window.

"I'm sure your cabin isn't that bad."

Inside the room, Julia kicked a leg high in the air as if auditioning for the Sugar Plum Fairy in *The Nutcracker*. If I tried out, I could be a girl who holds a Christmas present. Scratch that, I'd be one of the presents, like one of those kids dressed as a rock in the school play. You sit there crouched underneath a wooden box. With any luck, they'd cut a hole in the top where I could poke my head out.

I turned away from the window. "Our performance is a disaster."

"Do you want me to come to get you? Remember, Arizona State is only—"

"No, Mom." I remembered the poster on my cabin wall. *Great sacrifice*. "I have to do this."

"OK, but if you change your mind ..."

"I know, but I won't."

I looked back in the dance studio's window. Chloe leaned against the barre while Julia posed in the middle of the studio, her arms curved in front like she held a giant beach ball. Niki copied her in the back with a smaller deflating stance.

"Mom, I'd better get back to the disaster now acting as my scholarship-winning exposé. I'll talk to you later."

"I'm sure camp will get better. Love you."

"Love you too."

I tucked the phone back in my shorts' pocket. Better get back. I surely couldn't make the practice session any worse.

When I walked into the studio, Hannah pressed on the screen of Chloe's cell phone and Mozart's *Rondo Alla Turca* filled the room. My stomach churned. The song did not have good memories.

Julia spun in quick circles like her foot could drill into the wood at any moment. Niki, on the other hand, flopped along with the music, her head turned sideways. I followed her gaze to the practice room on the opposite side. The distraction made sense. Cutoff tees, crewcuts, and calves for days. A group of guys exhibited their athleticism during a practice session.

Julia leaped in Niki's transfixed direction, unaware of her picture-perfect toe sailing toward Niki's unaware body. The two collided, and by the time Mozart had played another bar, Julia and Niki were collapsed in a pile on the floor.

"What do you think you're doing?" Niki smacked the ground.

"I'm *dancing*. What are *you* doing?" Julia stood.

Niki turned to Hannah. "I tried ballet. Classical isn't working."

Chloe stood from the bench. "I agree. The music doesn't accentuate my voice."

"Girls, girls," Hannah interrupted. "There are other options we haven't thought of. Geri, you've been quiet. Do you have any ideas?"

All eyes turned toward me. Mom's offer to pick me up seemed pretty good right then, but I wanted to win the scholarship more. I closed my eyes. Think, self. Think. Did we stand out at anything? We had to have some talent.

"Sleeping is not a showstopper." Chloe's high-pitched voice disrupted my thought process.

"Give her a minute." Niki spoke an octave lower.

"Yes, let's give her all the time in the world. We have all day."

"It's been like thirty seconds, Chloe."

"Thirty seconds we've lost of precious practice time."

"We have a week." Nicole flayed her arms. "What're thirty seconds?"

Fighting. We would win gold at fighting. Could Niki and Chloe argue on stage? The conflict would be entertaining, but maybe Niki and *Julia* could battle their feelings out during our performance.

"I've got an idea." My eyes flashed open. "Let's do a battle."

"This is a talent show, not Comicon." Chloe clucked her tongue.

"No, a dance battle."

"I'm listening." Niki pursed her lips.

"Niki, you like hip-hop right? And, Julia, you like ballet. Why don't we choreograph a dance where you guys are battling back and forth?"

Julia tilted her head. "The idea could work. Do I get to win?"

"Seriously?" Niki looked at Julia.

"Geri, I love this idea!" Hannah applauded.

"Where do we fit in?" Chloe planted her hands on her hips.

"I haven't got there." I raised my eyebrows and bit my lip.

"Great." Chloe rolled her eyes.

"No worries." Hannah shrugged it off. "The thought's a great start. I'll book more time slots in this studio." She shot out the door and down the hall.

The plan was a start. Of *what* I wasn't too sure.

Reasons I Don't Like Camp–

7. **Teamwork**

Reasons I Like Camp–

2. **Ideas that almost sorta work**

CHAPTER 9

"¡*Eres genia!* You're a genius!" Abby's eyes grew another half-inch as she leaned forward on the white plastic table. The Snack Shack had the only non-wooden furniture in the whole camp. I fidgeted in a matching plastic chair. The sweat on the back of my legs suctioned to the seat.

Open windows lined the wall, and a huge circular fan droned back and forth in the corner. Its breeze blew the stray hairs from my ponytail around my face, and then the air left again all too soon. I cooled my palms on the cold glass of lemonade. At least some part of me survived the July heat.

"We don't have the whole thing figured out yet." I stared at the huge Camp Hi-Lu-Ma-Po sign on the wall. Perform to Shine. Ha. I needed to perform to survive.

"You have a good start. A battle between Julia and Niki is perfect." Abby took a sip of her lemonade.

"They're already good at fighting off stage."

"See? *No te preocupes*. The piece will come together." Abby grabbed my arm. "Don't look now, Geri, but your day is about to get a whole lot better."

"Do you see Chloe leaving with her oversize suitcase?" I took a bite of my sugar cookie.

Abby rolled her eyes.

"Hey, Abby. Hey, Geri."

The sound of his voice surprised me. I tried to say hello to Ethan, but I semi-choked instead, sending cookie crumbs across the table. Maybe he didn't see my mouth malfunction? Only if the table had been wooden and similar in color to the cookies. But, no.

Abby looked at me and scrunched her eyebrows. "Hey, Ethan."

With a small cough and a big swallow, I got the cookie down and turned around with my best I'm-a-normal-person face.

"Hi," I managed. My throat felt scratchy from swallowing oversized crumbs but healed at the sight of his cool blue eyes. So much better than a Ricola cough drop. He should always come around when I'm sick with a scratchy throat. Although, then I'm a mucus breeding tissue factory. Pass.

"You promised me a jam session today." Ethan tapped the guitar on his back. "Are you free now?"

"I ... um ..." I looked to Abby for help. I wanted to spend time alone with Ethan, but then I would be alone. With Ethan.

"Yes, actually, I need to get back to my cabin." Abby finished her lemonade and stood.

So much for a wing woman.

"What?" I looked at Abby like she was Vivaldi's last inhaler.

"Yeah, remember, I told you about that ... thing." She threw her cup in the trash. "Have fun *jammin'*. I'll see you guys later." She gave me a wink before leaving. And she didn't understand the second time either.

"Ready?" Ethan looked at me.

"Yeah," I tried my best to sound confident and followed him out the door.

Don't get me wrong, I was thrilled to spend time with Ethan, but now I would have to talk to him and *not* look like a fool.

"Music Studio's this way." He pointed in the opposite direction of the dance building.

I put my hands in the front pockets of my shorts. Real casual. Or too cowgirl? I took them out. They hung by my sides, and I realized Ethan did the same. Accidental touching warning. Decision made. Hands in pockets.

"What got you into music?" Ethan glanced at me.

I looked at the top of the large pine trees and gave myself a quick pep talk. He asked a simple question with a simple answer. I could do this.

"My parents put me in lessons before I could reach the piano bench. Been playing ever since. What about you?" I let out a deep breath but scrunched my lips together hoping he wouldn't hear.

"I didn't start playing more until recently. Don't get me wrong. I love the guitar, but music takes me away from all the arguing in my house. It helps add to the practice hours."

"I know what you mean. Chopin didn't play all his pieces *forte*, but—"

"The louder you play, the less you hear them." Ethan finished my thought.

"Exactly." I allowed myself to peek at him out of the corner of my eye. He got me. I could talk to him. And he was gorgeous. Were we in the enchanted forest and no one told me?

"Do you ever want to get away from it all?"

"Yeah, I used to, but my dad just moved out." I took my hands out of my pockets and clasped them in front of me.

Ethan's eyes softened. "I'm sorry."

I forced a smile. "Don't be. Life's better without him around." My stomach churned. Days were better without him around, but the new him, not the old him. I still missed *that* Dad.

"I don't know what I want. For my family to get fixed I guess, but a complete relationship repair needs a miracle."

Ethan pulled at the black straps of his guitar case. The instrument seemed to be weighing him down, or maybe he couldn't carry the load along with the parental tension. I wished I could take the burden for him, but I had my own heaviness.

Ethan took a deep breath. "Jesus said in Matthew all things are possible with him. If he could walk on water, he can help fix my parents. I have hope but believing is hard when you're in the middle of a mess."

If God could do all things, I agreed with Ethan on this one. I'd want my parents to be back together and happy, but could reconciliation happen after everything my dad had done? Could God erase things too?

"Seems impossible." I swallowed. "I don't know which one seems more hopeless. My parents getting back together or our cabin putting on something decent for the talent show."

Ethan chuckled. "You've got time to figure both out."

I wanted to tell him all about our mess of a talent show number and how his supposed ex-girlfriend added to the drama, but I didn't know where they stood. Even if they weren't together, they used to be. He wouldn't appreciate any Chloe bashing.

We reached the music building, and I held my breath before I stepped inside hoping for another air-conditioned space. A slow smile spread across my face as I entered the entryway. The welcome coolness enveloped me like an Artic hug. I'd be spending a lot of my time in refrigerated studios. Thank goodness.

Two practice rooms lined the beige wall on the left. To the right lay a carpeted hallway with a few more rooms forming an "L" shape. Even with the doors closed, the sound of a fierce piano could still be heard near the entryway.

"Let's check with the counselor to see if there's an open room." We walked down the hall and into an office.

A college-age counselor sat in front of a desk in his Camp Hi-Lu-Ma-Po shirt. He bobbed his disheveled hair to a silent beat.

"Excuse me." Ethan tapped on the door jamb.

The boy kept nodding his head and looking at the books in front of him. Small wires trailed down from his ears to a phone lying on the messy desk.

I pointed to them. "He has earbuds in."

"Excuse me!"

The boy drummed the silent beat on the table.

Ethan walked into the room and tapped him on the shoulder. "Hey, there!"

The guy jumped, turned around, and pulled the earbuds out. "Sorry. I kinda get lost in the music." He ruffled his sandy blond hair.

Ethan pointed to his guitar. "Is there a practice room free?"

The counselor picked up a clipboard from the top of a slew of papers. He ran his finger down the list. "Umm, yeah, the girl in five should be finishing up."

"Great. Thanks." I guess Ethan tried to smile, but his mouth didn't quite get there.

"No problem. I'm Tyler, if you need anything." He swiveled back around in his chair and popped the music back in his ear.

The floorboards squeaked as we walked back down the hall. We stopped when we found a room with a white five hanging at the top of the door. Ethan reached for the handle but the door opened on its own.

Chloe's pretty face appeared. Her eyes bulged and looked back and forth between me and Ethan before inspecting me for my spotted coat possibilities. I didn't have the usual black and white spots Cruella prefers. Mosquito bites will have to do, Ms. de Vil.

She pushed up the left sleeve of her black sweater. "Ethan. Geraldine. What a nice surprise." I squinted and took a step back. Chloe scrunched the right sleeve but stopped herself. Instead, she let the left side down.

"Hey, Chloe," Ethan tried his grin. Again. "Are you finished? We don't want to kick you out."

"Umm ... yeah. Are you guys practicing?" She tightened her ponytail.

"I don't know if you would call it practicing." Ethan stepped past her into the room, his guitar grazing her pretty blonde head. "But ya know, jammin' a bit."

"Right. Jammin'." Her eyes darted between Ethan and me again. "*Together*?" She picked the word off the floor and hurled the letters at me.

I followed Ethan into the room. My heart beat in my chest, but I would take nervous scary over a Chloe-Cruella-making-me-into-a-mosquito-bite-coat type of scary.

Ethan put his guitar on the floor next to a worn piano. "Yes, Chloe. People play music together all the time. It's called a duet."

Chloe faced us and plodded her wedges backward through the doorway. "Right. A duet." She flashed a smile that would have scared the toughest dalmatian before turning and walking away. Had I awoken a beautiful monster?

CHAPTER 10

Our "jam session" had ended a while ago, but I still couldn't wipe the aggravating smile off my face. Warmth radiated in my heart, but my brain stood by with a fire extinguisher. Those flames needed to be put out. Men couldn't be trusted.

Trying to hide my real feelings from Abby mirrored trying to hide Vienna from Beethoven.

"Geri, you've been quiet long enough. You have to give me every detail." Abby twirled down the dirt path. "I see a smile on your face. Time with Ethan had to be amazing!"

I forced the corners of my mouth to droop and kept walking, staring straight ahead. "I already told you. Practice went fine."

Abby frowned. "Fine is not acceptable. What's with you? This is Ethan we're talking about. The same Ethan you couldn't stop staring at the first day of camp, and you got to spend the whole afternoon together. I thought you would be elated."

"Elated?"

"Yes. *Feliz*. Happy. Enthusiastic. Not whatever this is."

I thought back to a few hours ago. Abby's words fell short. Playing music with Ethan hadn't been amazing. It had been regrettably fantastic. Our music had blended better than Beethoven and his wig. Or would that not be saying much?

The tall pines stood like black statues in front of the pink evening sky. The setting sun traced lines of orange and purple through the landscape. Another day in paradise.

Or pandemonium.

Figuring out a direction for our performance had been a small win, even though we still needed to implement the idea. But then these growing feelings for Ethan. They needed to be squelched.

I took a deep breath. “I don’t want to get my hopes up. Guys aren’t worth the hassle. They let you down in the end.”

Abby put her arm around my shoulder. “Not every guy is like your dad, Geri.”

“I know.” I crossed my arms. “But what if *he* is?”

“What if *he’s* not?”

We turned the corner and saw huddled campers surrounding the dancing flame fire pits. The log benches had been moved to circle them. The smell of burning wood drifted to my nose. Bonfires might be a good thing about camp.

“You should give him a chance. And you know what else you should give a chance?”

“What?”

“Marshmallows.” She squeezed my shoulder before letting go and pulled me to a nearby table. The display looked like an exploded s’mores factory. Bags of marshmallows piled high on one side with boxes of graham crackers and chocolate bars on the others.

“Ouch!” A sharp pain struck my ankle. I reached down and picked up the pointed metal culprit.

“*Buen trabajo*, Geri. We needed a roasting stick for the marshmallows.”

Leave it to Abby to find the good in everything. I wished I had positivity like her.

“Fork holders are in charge of marshmallows. I’ll get the chocolate and graham crackers.”

I reached into the bag of puffy white treats, but my hand ran into someone else. "Sorry." I pulled back and tucked my hair behind my ear.

"No problem." It took me about 0.2 seconds to realize the deep voice belonged to Ethan.

"Ladies first." He flashed his faint-worthy smile.

"Thanks." I reached a shaky hand in the bag.

"How do you like yours roasted?"

"Golden brown," I actually replied without stuttering. "Gooey on the inside and crispy on the outside." I'd answered Ethan quicker than a mosquito goes for type O blood, but I don't mess around when it comes to the most important part of the s'more.

"Allright then. Golden brown marshmallows coming right up." Ethan winked.

I looked down and hoped the darkness would cover the flush coming over my cheeks.

"I like them burned." He grabbed a white—for the time being—puff.

"Got the marshmallows, Geri?" Abby appeared next to me. "And Ethan," she added a little too peppy.

"Hey, Abby," Ethan gave her a head bob.

"Any open seats next to you guys?" She looked at me with conniving saucer eyes.

"Yeah, we'll make space."

"Great." Abby slid herself in front of two roasting forks lying on the table, hiding them with her back. "And we have a stick to share." She lifted her eyebrows and peered at me.

I raised mine at her.

"You can thank me later," Abby whispered in my ear. Thank her, or maybe poke her with the roasting fork.

We followed Ethan to one of the campfires. When he said he thought they could fit a couple more, he must have meant a couple of kindergarteners. An open seat remained on the left and about one and a half free spots on the other side.

Abby sprinted to the log on the left with a medal-worthy speed, leaving the spot and a half for me and Ethan. The bench stood as our own rustic loveseat. Although, we weren't in love, and I'm not sure I'd qualify the space as a seat.

Ethan sat down first and I followed, well, half of me did. The other half perched on an imaginary extension of the log. Both Abby and Ethan's neighbor engaged in conversation, leaving me on my own with him. Again.

"You're up first." Ethan held up the stick.

"Yeah, sure." I hoped I wouldn't be roasting first if I fell off the log.

Ethan handed me the stick, and I put the marshmallows on the spokes. I leaned forward but the fire's heat attacked my face. I stretched my arm as far as the muscle would go without pulling the bone out of the socket and tilted my head away from the fiery flames. First, I sweltered during the day. Then, I roasted at night.

"You want help?"

"I've got this." I tried to turn my head toward the fire to look like a normal marshmallow-roasting person but squinted while trying to keep my eyes from smoldering.

"I don't think so." Ethan reached for the roasting fork. His thumb brushed over my fingers, and I dropped the stick into the fire. The marshmallows didn't stand a chance.

"Whoops." I wished the heat would evaporate the raindrops tickling the inside of my stomach. "Sorry."

"No need to apologize. Guess those are mine." Ethan picked up the roasting fork and blew out the charred puffy, gooey treat.

Ethan waved the burned culprits in the air before popping one into his mouth. He held the other out to me.

"This is how I like them. Wanna try one?"

"No, thanks." I shook my head. "I'll take my chances with Round Two."

He put the scorched treat on a graham cracker instead. "You helped me with my s'more. I'm going to return the favor." Ethan put new marshmallows on the fork and leaned in close to the fire. His face must have been heat resistant or maybe it didn't matter because he was so hot already.

"I'm glad we got to jam today." Ethan smiled but kept his focus on the browning goo.

"Definitely." Like Beethoven and his wig.

"Sometimes I forget music is fun instead of an escape." Ethan stared into the fire, the flames reflecting in his eyes.

"I know what you mean." I followed his gaze. The embers glowed in the darkness, their surrounding flames dancing in the night sky. I took a deep breath, the smell of burning wood coming with the night air. My lungs and stomach settled.

"Has your cabin got anywhere with your piece for the talent show?" Ethan's voice broke me out of the flickering trance.

"We have an idea." I turned to him, feeling more relaxed and ready to give the whole conversation thing a try.

"Oh, yeah?"

"Imagine hip-hop and ballet combined into one piece." I shifted on the log. My thigh muscles burned from holding half of myself up. Should have spent more time doing squats in gym class last spring.

"Where would you come in?"

"Maybe playing the music for their dance."

"Do you have a song?" Ethan turned the swelling marshmallow, its edge revealing a golden brown.

I shook my head. "No."

Ethan lifted the roasting stick from the fire. "Why don't you write the music for your cabin's piece?"

My cheeks grew hot, and not from the fire. "I don't compose."

"Maybe not yet, but you killed it on the piano today. You should try creating harmonies."

"I don't know."

Ethan leaned the roasting fork against the log, the roasted puffs reaching to the sky. He waved one in the air before breaking off a small piece and holding the gooey treat in front of my face. "Try it." He brought the sticky threat closer. "Or else."

"Or else what?"

He lifted his eyebrows, and a sly grin spread across his lips. "You know."

"You wouldn't." I searched his face trying to decide whether he was the type of guy capable of food face-smashing but grew distracted by his sparkling blue eyes. I had my answer when a toasty marshmallow kissed my cheek.

The warmth of the sugary glop matched the glow in my heart. That's how you know you've fallen hard. When guys do annoying things, but you find them endearing, like white goop on your face.

"I warned you," Ethan grinned.

He warned me about the marshmallow, but no one told me about this, this cute guy I'd undoubtedly fall for at camp.

I peeled the sticky treat off my cheek. "I need a napkin."

Ethan stood. "I'll get one."

"No, no. You need to make my s'more. You owe me."

Ethan smiled and sat back down. "Deal."

I walked over to the s'more factory table. The marshmallow scene counted as flirting, right? The concept remained foreign to me due to the lack of male attention in my life. I scrubbed my face with a napkin and smiled. I liked flirting. Then, I turned around to see the worst thing on the Camp Hi-Lu-Ma-Po planet.

The beautiful monster had taken over my kindergartener spot next to Ethan. Why did she *not* look awkward sitting there? Oh, because she basically sat in his lap. She put her dainty claw on his shoulder and tousled her other hand through his caramel hair.

I toyed with the idea of going back over there to claim my half-log spot back when Chloe claimed hers. She kissed him. Right then and there.

My eyes grew warm, and I turned around as quickly as I could, throwing the napkin on the table. I needed to escape, to get away before Cruella snatched anything else precious to me. The pain traced back to me. I let him in. Guys couldn't be trusted.

I ran to the cabin trying to dump Ethan from my mind. Cleaning the cafeteria. *Dump*. Playing music. *Dump*. Kissing the Chloe Monster. *Big dump*.

I had bigger things to worry about. The scholarship. That's what I needed to focus on. The scholarship.

CHAPTER 11

The perfect piano solo is supposed to be like a banana split, a steady base of notes and chords topped with the sweetness of passion and gusto. My piano solo resembled a banana split with pickles, sour and tainted from parental noise.

My fingers hit the piano keys. B. A. G#. A. C. "Can't we move on?"

My father's notes.

D. C. B. C. E. "I don't believe you!"

Mom's beat.

F. E. D#. "I've apologized!"

Father's *animato*.

E. B. A. "Words aren't enough."

Mom's *accelerando*.

G#. My father's *staccato*.

A. Mom's *crescendo*.

B. A. G. A. C. C. C. C. My forehead pounding on the piano replaced Mozart in the practice room, adding to my misery. I'd slept horribly after turning into a pathetic weeping blob in my bunk last night, and now I had a resounding headache as payment for the tears.

Officially dating or not officially dating, titles didn't matter. Chloe had kissed Ethan, and he had let her. There had to be something there, and I needed to stay out of any more complicated relationships.

I stood and walked over to the nearby window. The sun shone through the openings in the pine trees. The bottom of the forest glowed while hints of darkness still resided at the top. I needed a little ray of sunshine. Or a big ray.

Chloe's mission to suck the good out of my life—literally—fell short of a deeper pain. Seeing her with Ethan brought back flashbacks of my parents' downfall. Mozart's notes accompanied the memories of the last time I played the piece. The day my dad left.

Mozart. Elgar. Vivaldi. I leaned my head against the white wall and slid down the wooden paneling until I reached the worn gray carpet. *Rondo Alla Turca* would be perfect for Julia's solo, and she'd already been dancing to the melody. The song also showcased my talent for the scholarship.

Distressing flashbacks stained the beauty of the piece. Thoughts of my cheating father now collided with the image of the monster taking her prey, but I needed the scholarship. The memories would have to go.

I went back to the piano and put my fingers on the keys. The sheet music didn't say *forte* but I pounded out the notes.

B. A. G#. A. C. Blondie must go.

D. C. B. C. E. I need to win the show.

Fortissimo.

F. Get out.

E. Camp's not about ...

D#. Chloe.

E. Or Ethan.

"Dude, are you trying to kill the piano?" Tyler stepped through the doorway wearing sage green board shorts and a gray Camp Hi-Lu-Ma-Po shirt. "And at this time? You're like the dawn patrol for pianists."

"The what?"

"You're playing so early in the morning."

"Sorry, I didn't know you'd be here already." I fidgeted on the piano bench. At least he couldn't hear my original lyrics. That would have been way more embarrassing.

Tyler leaned against the doorway, his wet hair a shade darker than yesterday. "No worries. You know what they say. Early bird gets the protein shake."

I scrunched my eyebrows.

Tyler waved his hand. "Never mind." He took a few steps toward the piano, and the light reflected off a black key necklace hanging over his T-shirt. "What's your name again?"

"Geri."

"Geri, if you're playing this early, you must not be messing around with the camp's talent show."

"Nope." I straightened the sheet music. "Our cabin needs to look good. I need to win the college scholarship."

"A scholarship applicant in the flesh."

He walked over to the piano and picked up the sheet music. "You guys doin' Mozart?"

"For the first section. We haven't figured out the other part yet. The song needs to be original."

"Have you got anything started?" He ran a hand through his disheveled hair. "You should make the dynamics *forte* and *fortissimo*. You're good at loud notes."

Tyler handed me the papers, but I missed. Mozart fell to the floor.

Ethan believed I could write music, but how much worth did his opinion hold? The totality of a burned marshmallow and Chloe's passed-down cherry Chapstick? No, thanks.

Tyler bent down to pick up the pages. "I wrote a killer piece last semester."

I took the music from him. "Really? You compose?"

"When I'm not surfing, I'm in the fine halls of UC Santa Barbara creating harmonies. I'm a music theory and composition major."

"Awesome. I'm just starting." I tucked a piece of hair behind my ear. "Or thinking of starting."

"Writing music is a great space to get into. I love playing other people's stuff, but when you compose, you're creating the masterpiece. The tune can be whatever you want."

Could I also orchestrate my life? Win the camp scholarship. Get into Juilliard. Become a concert pianist. There. Done.

"I don't know about whatever I want, but my cabin needs music to match our number for the talent show."

"Sounds like a good challenge."

I thought back to the cabin fighting earlier. "Yeah, the piece is a challenge all right."

Tyler fiddled with low-pitch notes on the piano, and the smell of his tangerine shampoo filled the space around the keys. "You want help?"

I could use all the help I could get. "Sure."

"I'll grab paper from the office and be right back. We're old school around here. Not much tech in these parts." Tyler gestured to the pine trees out the window before walking out the door.

I took a deep breath and looked at the bars of music in front of me. I was not Wolfgang Amadeus Mozart, but I was Geraldine Valeri Bruchi. I could write music. I needed to write music.

Tyler walked back in with staff paper and sharpened pencils. He motioned for me to scoot over and sat on the bench.

"All right, what are we creating?"

"Our cabin is performing a battle—ballet vs. hip-hop. I'm using this for the ballet part." I pointed to *Rondo Alla Turca*. "But we need music for the hip-hop portion."

"Hip-hop piano. Love the idea. It's different."

"Good different?"

Tyler smiled. "Yeah, these judges like originality. What are you thinking?"

I picked up one of the pencils and tapped the eraser on the piano. With my eyes closed, I could see Niki center stage.

"Something with determination." I played an eerie chord with my left hand. "Maybe A minor."

Tyler nodded. "I like the sound."

"Maybe start with the *E* chords, like Niki's own version of walk-out music."

For the next half hour, Tyler helped me record an intro for Niki's solo. I felt refocused, determined, unware of the Chloe monster. Cruella can attack, but Dalmatians can also fight.

CHAPTER 12

I felt as determined as Ana to get Elsa back and save the kingdom—or the cabin. Only Flagstaff radiated heat instead of ice, and I needed to eat first. Composing works up an appetite.

When I entered the dining hall, the line held a few sleepy campers. The cafeteria worker plopped mushy French toast sticks and tater tots on my tray. Before heading to a table, I grabbed an orange to balance out the fried unhealthiness.

I spotted my cabin, well most of them, and sat down next to Niki. No sign of Cruella. Maybe she snuck off to torment more puppies.

Niki turned to look at me. "Girl, where have you been?"

I slid the sheet music in front of her. "Helping us win."

She looked at the papers. "What's this?"

"Your music for our piece, the beginning anyway."

Hannah turned toward us. "Geri, you scared me. We wanted to start a search party, right girls?"

"Right after this French toast." Niki took a bite of her syrup-drenched breakfast.

"Sorry. I woke up early. Thought I'd get a head start on our music."

Hannah's face softened. "All right, but don't disappear again. Let me see what you've got there."

She took the paper and looked the notes over. Her eyes moved back and forth as she nodded her head. “This is good, Geri, really good. You did this?”

“I had help, but yeah. And Julia, I know how to play *Rondo Alla Turca*, the music you used yesterday. I think this could work once I get further along with the piece.”

Niki patted me on the back “Good work, Geri.”

“As long as I have my classical music.” Julia straightened her already perfect posture.

Hannah smiled. “See, girls, I knew we would work it out.”

“What has been worked out?” Chloe set her breakfast next to Julia. The tray held a fruit bowl, a piece of toast, and an overcooked hardboiled egg. A rancid stench circled her. Did the odor belong to the egg or her vibes?

“Geri is going to play and write the music for our performance.” Hannah smiled.

“Perfect. Sounds like a piano *solo* is well suited for her.” Chloe popped a grape into her devious mouth.

I bit my tongue rather than sticking it out at her. I had more important things to fill my mind and my days. Hannah stood. “Practice starts in fifteen, girls. Let’s get going.”

The dance studio mirrors reflected the perturbed look on my face. I wanted to get back in the music studio, but Hannah had insisted we “stay together as a team.” My rear ached from sitting and watching Niki and Julia dance on the unforgiving wood floor. Sitting next to the Lock-kiss Monster added to my misery.

“Let’s try the number from the top.” Hannah motioned to the dancers.

“Practice isn’t the same without the real music.” Niki stretched her arms across her chest.

"Geri is working on the piece. Plus watching probably gives her inspiration."

I fidgeted on the wooden dance floor. "Right. Inspiration."

Hannah clapped twice. "Let's start, Geri."

I attended to my super important job, pushing play for the track. Niki leaned against one of the bars on the wall while her counterpart took center stage. Julia lifted her leg to start the dance I'd seen a dozen times by now. *Pas de boureé*. Julia leaned and crossed her feet underneath her. *Chassé. Saut de chat.* She slid to the side and jumped in the air. The terms were ingrained in my mind after hearing her repeat them aloud over and over again.

"I get inspired too. From other people." Chloe turned toward me. "Other campers. Like when I heard a motivating duet in the music studio." Chloe's ice blue eyes bubbled with mischief. Conniving lip vacuum. Did she know I saw her kiss Ethan?

"Or sometimes weird things provoke me. Like marshmallows or s'mores or bonfires."

She definitely knew I saw.

"Isn't it time for a break?" I shouted over the music.

I wiped my clammy forehead even though the air conditioning hummed from the studio's vents. The drama proved too much. I didn't know how to deal with man-stealing villains.

"We'll take a break when we've earned one." Julia twirled in circles.

After the past few days, I had earned a break for life.

"Geri!" I turned to see Niki moving toward the center of the floor. "The music."

"Sorry." I pressed pause.

The studio door clicked open. Ethan walked into the room.

Faster than an Eggo pops out of a toaster, Chloe jumped off the floor and ran behind me. I dared not turn around to see the Lock-Kiss with her prey again.

At least Niki's lack of music made eavesdropping easy. "Chloe, we talked about this last night. I need to talk to—"

"I know, but we can still—"

"Chloe, no. I'm sorry."

I heard footsteps. "Geri." His voice called from behind me. I closed my eyes and clicked my tennis shoes three times. The motion should take me home, right, Dorothy and Toto? Maybe not home, but somewhere else. *Anywhere* else.

The floor creaked as someone sat beside me. I opened my eyes and saw black flip-flops instead of tall wedges. Great. I even preferred to see Chloe's pink manicured toes over Ethan's feet.

"Can we talk about what happened?" Ethan leaned to peer into my downcast eyes.

"This is a closed practice, Ethan." Julia slammed her fists to her hips.

I looked at her. "Your turn." I played her music once again and the beauty of Mozart filled the stifling air.

I watched Julia dance. "There's nothing to talk about."

"If there was nothing to talk about, you wouldn't be mad."

"I'm not mad."

"Then why won't you look at me?"

To prove him wrong, I did look at him. Big mistake. My heart melted as soon as I saw those sparkling blue eyes. A few inches lower, however, lay his mouth, his deceitful mouth.

I scrunched my forehead. "You kissed her."

Ethan reached for my arm, but I drew my hand back.

"She kissed me, but I reminded her we're over. Being her ex doesn't mean she has the right to kiss me anytime she wants."

I wanted to believe him, but the past had told me differently. Men shouldn't be trusted.

I shook my head and stood. "Look. It doesn't matter. We weren't anything anyway."

"But, Geri—"

I took a step back. "Don't."

I picked up my tote bag and fled. Where? I didn't know. My feet ran down the faded hall and out into the blazing sunshine. The pounding of my sneakers blocked out the sound of Mozart I'd left behind.

Reasons I Don't Like Camp—

8. Beautiful monsters who kiss

CHAPTER 13

My feet ended up taking shelter in the music studio and so did my heart. I paced up and down the halls, too nervous to sit still, but too anxious to do anything productive.

Why did I have to make such a scene? Storming out of the dance studio like Handel fleeing an out-of-tune orchestra. If Chloe's goal included getting to me, then she prevailed with glistening colors.

"Back so soon?" Tyler stood in the office doorway.

I squeezed my hands together trying to calm myself. "I needed to get away from practice."

"Going that well, huh?" Tyler raised his eyebrows.

"Let's keep working on the piece from this morning."

Tyler smiled. "Composing is growing on you then."

Anything to distract me would have been growing on me then. Edvard Grieg's lucky frog would grow on me if it got me away from the Ethan-Chloe drama.

"Room Five is open." Tyler pointed down the hall.

"Any others?" I asked, not wanting to be reminded of an earlier jam session.

Tyler squinted but didn't press me. "One?"

I marched down the hall to the first room and burst through the door. Even the spider web in the corner and the smell of stale fries in the trash couldn't stop me.

"And this is why I suggested Five. I haven't got around to cleaning this one today." Tyler followed me into the room.

"A spotless room doesn't matter. We have a piano. We have music. We have brains. That's all we need to get this done."

"Remind me to never get in your way."

I dumped my tote bag on the floor and pulled out the beginning of the song Tyler and I had started earlier. I slammed the paper on the music's piano stand, but one piece only makes so much noise. I dropped the pencil for a melodramatic effect, and the wood clinked against the metal. Business time.

"Do you want me to get you bubble wrap, maybe a blown-up balloon to pop?"

I straightened the music. "No, this is good. Let's start."

"Are you sure you're OK?"

OK like I avoided madness over stupid Chloe and her stupid conquering lips? No. OK like I refrained from falling over dead at the age of fifteen? Yes.

"Yeah, just got some stuff going on. Digging into music helps me get my mind off the chaos."

Tyler nodded and settled on the piano bench next to me. "We're starting in A minor, right?"

I placed my fingers on A-C-E and released the eerie sound into the quiet practice room. "Sounds like Niki."

"Good, that's what we're going for. Remind me what we had."

The first few bars floated through the practice room, a mixture of A and D Minor Chords flowing through quarter and half notes. I envisioned Niki making her grand entrance, a confident smirk on her face.

Tyler mimicked the chords on his board shorts and bobbed his head to the *grave* beat. For a moment, I lost him in the serious tone of the music. He closed his eyes and swayed back and forth with the change in each chord.

I played the last bar we'd written, and Tyler paused before popping his eyes open. "And now we *accelerando*. Let's add an intense melody. I'll play our A minor chords, and you play a matching tune."

He moved to the other side of the bench near the bass clef notes, and I scooched over to the higher notes. Tyler's left hand hit the keys and his imaginary beat came to life. I placed my fingers on the piano, but they remained frozen.

"Go ahead, Geri. Whatever comes to mind. Creativity doesn't have to be perfect."

My thumb hit the A an octave higher than Tyler's chord. The note didn't sound bad, balanced out the deepness of the minor chord. I hit the A again, and again, and again. Inspiration plummeted. I imagined Niki curling up in a round ball on the floor. I'd failed her.

"There are other notes ya know."

I knew he wanted to lighten the mood, but the air remained heavy.

Tyler patted my shoulder. "You're thinking too much. Close your eyes."

I obeyed even though I felt awkward. Desperation makes you put up with embarrassment.

"We're writing this for Niki." Tyler played our first few bars. "She's in the middle of the stage, getting ready to take Julia on."

Double-A minor. D minor. Double-A minor. D minor.

I could see Niki, dressed in black, ready to fight.

Double-A minor. D minor. Double-A minor. D minor.

She lifted her hands to the sky and spread her arms, taking a fighting position.

Double-A minor. D minor. Double-A minor. D minor.

Tyler placed my thumb on the A. *A-A-A.*

Niki's left darted to the right. *F-E-D. F-E-D.*

My right hand danced along the piano while Niki soared in my mind. When I wanted her to move faster, I played eighth notes. When the time came for her to slow down, I changed the beat to quarter notes. Imaginary Niki completed a high jump before crouching on the floor. I popped my eyes open.

Tyler moved his hands from the keys. “And that, campers, is the beginning of an epic song.”

“How will I ever be able to play the same tune again?”

Tyler held up his phone. “The miracle of recordings.”

“But how did you –”

Tyler smiled. “You got the musician look. I figured taping the session couldn’t hurt.”

The recording held melodic promise. We spent the next half hour replaying and copying the tune on Tyler’s phone.

“Looks like we need more paper,” Tyler added a string of eighth notes to the last bar. “I’ll be right back.”

He walked out of the room leaving me with the piano and fresh piece. I studied the composition. We had done this. I had done this. I breathed a sigh of relief. At least my musical side of life recovered, even if my personal life continued to drown.

“Geri?” Hannah’s voice sounded near the front door.

“In here.”

Hannah’s tight face softened when she saw me. “Oh, thank goodness. I didn’t know what had happened to you.”

“I ...” Trying to explain the whole situation to Hannah seemed daunting. And silly.

Hannah joined me on the piano bench. “I know our piece isn’t great right now, but we’ll get there.” She pointed to the music on the piano. “And look what an awesome start you have.”

“Hannah Banana.” Tyler entered the room holding a pile of papers.

"Is Tyler the help you've been getting?"

"More like mentoring," Tyler shrugged. "This girl has got skill."

My cheeks felt warm. "I don't know about that."

"Did you know she's entering the scholarship competition?" Tyler placed the staff paper on the piano.

Hannah smiled. "I did. Learned her main goal when we first met. I'm proud of you, Geri—working like a champ. A lot of students use this camp as more of a vacation, but not you. You're determined to succeed."

I didn't have a choice. I needed to get the scholarship to go to Juilliard and get away from my crazy family or be miserable for the next four years.

"Thanks," I pressed my lips together. I didn't feel like explaining my predicament.

Hannah stood. "I'll let you keep at it. Just wanted to check in. We'll see you in the cafeteria for dinner."

Tyler replaced Hannah on the bench. "Now, where were we?"

I positioned my hands on the piano. "Writing a killer piece for our cabin."

Reasons I like Camp–

3. *Becoming a composer*

CHAPTER 14

My heart sped as fast as a violin playing the *Flight of the Bumblebee*. This could not be happening. Teambuilding is fun, they say. Pushing yourself helps you grow, they say.

They lie.

I didn't have to grow. I'd be dead soon. On that course. Any moment.

I clung to a rough rope hanging forty feet above the air and looked straight ahead. The course wound like a snake through the forest with no end in sight. A thick cable strung the whole nightmare together, resembling a laundry line with the campers being the ill-fated clothes hanging from the rope. The sun had dried me. You can take me down now.

A breeze rattled the tall trees surrounding the high-ropes course, their leaves swishing with laughter at the panic-stricken girl on the line.

"C'mon, Geri. You can do it." Hannah shouted from a faraway wooden platform.

I stood in the middle of a skill-building challenge. Confidence. Perseverance. I needed those skills. Collaboration—I could do without. Brahms stayed single.

The wooden plank supporting my feet seemed to be getting smaller by the second. The next one loomed supposedly within walking distance, maybe for a giant. The rope dangled in front of me, but I remained frozen with a credible fear. A fear I would fall while Chloe did her Cruella laugh as my helpless body plummeted to the ground.

Chloe's investment in the activity fell off the course a long time ago. She had yet to take her turn and stood next in line on the podium. Her compact mirror and reflecting image seemed way too important. Yes, please take the time to inspect yourself while I face death.

"C'mon, girl. You got this," Niki shouted.

Mozart. Beethoven. Bach. Soothing words didn't work this time.

"Getting to the next block is simple, Geri." Julia gestured from the end of the course. "Reach up and take the rope. At the same time—"

"Julia. You're not helping." I closed my eyes.

"Sorry. If you would like to dangle there all day, go right ahead."

She made completing the course look easy with her embedded balletic balance. Her feet had superhero powers and could turn any which way they wanted.

"Maybe you guys should go on ahead." The rope burned into my hand.

"We're not going to leave you behind." Hannah gave me a stern-teacher glare.

"You're making me more nervous all standing there staring at me."

"Girls, turn around." Hannah circled her finger in the air.

In the next few seconds, I stared at the back of Niki's black T-shirt, Hannah's staff shirt, and Julia's yoga tank top. I glanced down to the ground below. This would never work.

"You got this, Geri." Ethan's voice sailed along the course.

Why didn't the tree branches take me then?

The rope swayed and in an unfortunate moment, Ethan stood right behind me.

I turned my head. "What are you doing here?"

His eyes brought comfort, but not enough.

"C'mon. You got this."

"I don't need your help."

"Your other option is to heist a piano up here and play an air solo. Maybe you'll win the scholarship for creative license."

His statement rang both true and irritating. I'm not sure which made me more determined, needing to get the course over with to win the scholarship or needing to prove Ethan wrong, but all of a sudden, my foot moved. My toes found the next block, and I lifted myself onto the platform. Two more to go.

The rope swayed and again Ethan landed behind me. "Good. Now step again." And I did. And one more time. My feet landed with a grateful thud on the wooden podium.

Hannah whipped around and hugged me. "I knew you could do it, Geri. Nice teamwork, Ethan."

Julia and Niki also turned around, but without the force of a torpedo. Niki patted me on the back. "Way to go, girl. Knew you would get here eventually."

Julia put her hands on her hips. "I'm glad you survived to share your musical talents."

Typical Julia. Mission on the brain.

Hannah turned to Chloe who lingered on the other side of the rope. "You're up, Chloe."

Chloe bolted on a mission to get to the other side. The last of the puppies huddled on a podium, and she needed to grasp us before we escaped.

"Nice work, Chloe," Hannah yelled. "Niki, why don't you get started on the next one?"

While Julia and Niki started the next course, Chloe continued with her puppy vendetta. She had a foot on the last platform when she slipped. She caught the rope above her head with her right arm, and the sleeve of her black sweater slid down.

A burn scar twisted from her wrist to the tip of her elbow. The pink bubbly stripe stood out against her otherwise flawless skin.

Chloe gasped, got her footing, and pushed down the sleeve of her sweater. I turned around to see if anyone else had seen the wound. Niki had begun the next course, and Hannah and Julia cheered her on.

Ethan squeezed my shoulder. "Good recovery, Chloe. You got this." I wanted to slough his hand away, but the warmth provided comfort for the sinking feeling in my stomach.

Chloe took her last step and joined us on the platform. For the first time, I saw humanity in her eyes. The color no longer resembled a blue sapphire, the cuts and edges causing a puzzle, but instead a clear blue sky. I cleared my throat. "Nice job, Chloe."

She tightened her ponytail and the curl at the tip bounced off her black defense shield. Clouds formed in her blue-sky eyes. The war resumed.

"Someone had to show you how to dominate the course. I get manicures in less time than it took you to move onto that platform, and they're deluxe."

Of course they are. My body felt confused. My cheeks raged with humiliation while my heart filled with sadness for the glimpse of the vulnerable girl I had seen.

Her stormy eyes found mine, and she took Ethan's hand. The sympathy I felt melted as the temperature on my cheeks elevated.

"Chloe, no." Ethan pulled back. "We're friends like I told you last night, but nothing more." He glanced at me. "You can't just kiss me and stuff."

"I didn't think you meant it." She bounced her finger on Ethan's nose.

So, nothing existed between them?

Ethan took a step back from Chloe. "I did."

Chloe pulled at the sleeves of her sweater and crossed her arms. "Fine." She turned toward the next obstacle. Niki, Julia, and Hannah waited on the other side. She grabbed the rope then swung through the trees.

"Geri," Ethan touched my shoulder again.

I felt safer with my feet on solid wood, although the height of the platform could be shorter. But I did not feel safe from him.

He took my hand, but I instantly stepped backward.

Ethan let go of my hand. "Careful. We're still on the platform."

I crossed my arms. "Right." On a tiny square in midair next to my arch enemy and a guy who maybe likes me. *Too much.*

"I meant it. Chloe and I are just friends."

I bit my bottom lip. "Friends. Note taken."

"Chloe and I are friends. You and I are—"

"Going on to the next course," I interrupted him. I couldn't face whatever relationship we had. I chose the high ropes instead of Ethan professing interest. I must be sick.

Ethan raised an eyebrow. "Right." He put his hands on his hips. "Let's get started then."

I took a step onto the next frightening adventure. Which held more fear—swaying ropes forty feet above the ground or letting Ethan into my heart?

Reasons I Don't Like Camp–

1. **Bugs**
2. **Cabin assignment mix-ups**
3. **Chloe**

4. *Talent shows without Abby*
5. ~~*Chloe with Ethan again*~~
6. *Chloe in my cabin*
7. *Teamwork*
8. *Beautiful monsters who kiss*
9. *High ropes courses*

CHAPTER 15

"You can't be mad at him forever." Abby kicked a rock along the dirt path while we walked to the music studio. She'd been trying to convince me to forgive Ethan, but easier said than done. I'd let him in, and he let me down. Like my dad had done to my mom.

"Sure, I can." I hugged the folder holding my scholarship essay.

"But he already explained everything."

"So?"

"So ..." Abby stopped walking and grabbed my arms. "This is simple, Geri. *Déjalo.* Forget the stupid kiss and move on. Ethan likes *you*."

I rolled my eyes. "Careful. My scholarship essay is in this folder."

"You have the paper in military-grade plastic. Stop trying to change the subject."

I hugged the essay tight and kept walking, pretending to be interested in the path's massive trees. But they held bugs. And bugs bite. And—

"Geri," Abby interrupted my ... thinking about nothing.

I faced her. "What do you want me to say?"

"That you'll forgive and give him another chance."

No. Chance given. Chance ruined. I held out my folder to Abby. "I didn't come here for boys. I came here for the scholarship."

"*Yo sé*. I know. but can't Ethan be an added bonus?" Abby raised her eyebrows.

"He kissed her, Abby, after we hung out." My chest felt tight. "I don't want him to be like my—"

Abby put her hand on my back. "He's not."

I shook my head and picked up the pace. "C'mon, I need to turn this in."

The music studio came into view. The competition mattered. Not boys.

Abby let out a heavy sigh. "At least you've got *determinación* going for you."

"I'll take that as a compliment."

We reached the building and stepped inside. An out-of-tune trumpet bellowed through the entryway. Abby grimaced, and I laughed. Good thing they decided to practice.

I motioned down the hall. "The directions say to turn the essay into the office."

The open door revealed Tyler sitting in the same spot as the first time I met him, but without earbuds.

He turned around and smiled. "Hey, Geri."

"Hey, Tyler. I came to—"

Abby nudged me. "Aren't you going to introduce us?" I turned to Abby, and her eyes held as much anticipation as Cinderella when she tried on the glass slipper.

I furrowed my eyebrows. "Right, sure. This is my friend—"

Abby walked into the room and held out her hand. She leaned toward him. "I'm Abby, Geri's best friend. We do everything together. In fact, I'm the reason Geri came here in the first place."

Oh, boy, there she went. Tyler did have a cute dimple when he smiled. I hadn't paid too much attention before because of a certain guy that should not be named.

Tyler brushed a wisp of hair from his face before standing up and shaking her hand. "That's sick, Abby. Wish I could get more of my buddies to come. I'm Tyler."

"There are more of you?" Abby's eyes twinkled.

I elbowed her side.

She glared at me. "Ouch."

"Tyler—" I interrupted before Abby could swoon further. "I came to turn in my essay for the scholarship." I took my Juilliard ticket out of the folder and held the paper out to him.

"Right on." He took the essay from me. "You're going to be one tough contender. Plus, you're committed. Practicing at dawn, composing up a storm, and now turning in your essay *way* early."

"Geri's determined." Abby batted her eyelashes. "I, on the other hand, like to go with the flow. Relax, like maybe with a walk on the beach at night."

Tyler moved to the other side of the room to either put the essay away or create space for Abby since she hadn't left his side. Maybe both motivated his actions.

We needed to go. My best friend's mind approached mushy guy status. I'd seen her flirt with crushes before. A huge wave of embarrassment threatened to crash into her at any minute.

I grabbed Abby's hand. "Thanks a lot, Tyler. We've got to get going." I pulled Abby toward the door. "See ya later."

"Later." He tousled his hair, and the strands stuck up the opposite way.

I jerked Abby out of the room before she could respond.

"What are you doing?" she shout-whispered at me. "And why didn't you tell me about this guy? *Muy guapo*."

I dragged Abby down the hall and out the front door. "Because I didn't want you to make a fool of yourself like you just did."

Abby kicked a rock on the path. "I did not."

I batted my eyelashes and clasped my hands together. "Oh, Tyler, I love everything you do and say. And I love romantic walks on the beach." I put my hands to my side. "But I'm only fifteen, and you're in college so this is ridiculous."

"You're just jealous, because I'm a natural."

"Yeah, sure." I shoved her. "I don't think he's cute."

"Are you blind?" Abby's face melted. "Or do you only have *ojos* for Ethan?"

"I'm not thinking about Ethan anymore."

"Oh good, because here he comes." She pointed down the path.

My eyes grew wide. "What? Where?" I searched for a place to disappear. Wait, there couldn't be a better place to escape. A forest with thousands of trees surrounded us. I grabbed Abby's hand. "We've got to hide."

Abby flipped her dark braid over her shoulder. "Gotcha." A satisfied smirk grew across her face.

"Why would you do that?"

"To see if you care, because you do." She pointed at me.

"You are so irritating."

"And so right." She crossed her arms.

A high-pitch cackle bounced off the large pine trees and into my ears. Chloe and her three clones waltzed down the pathway, all four of their ponytails swinging to the same beat.

Abby followed my gaze. "Don't let them bother you, Geri. Remember, he told you he's not interested in her."

I watched them march their short skirts back toward the cabins. Maybe Ethan thought of Chloe as a friend, but she had more than amicability on her mind. I didn't need to enter into a guy war. Plus, with supermodel legs, she had an unfair advantage.

Abby *chasséd* down the path. “When are you composing with Tyler again? I’m thinking I could come and be moral support. And bring snacks. My mom says the way to a man is through his stomach. I wonder what he likes. Buttery popcorn or ...”

While Abby danced and planned out her mission to get Tyler to notice her, I let my thoughts float to Ethan. Did I care as much as Abby said I did? Could I allow myself to trust him?

Dusk approached and the mosquitos grew vicious. I slapped one on my arm. *Ouch*. Did the pain foreshadow the hurt to come if I let Ethan in?

CHAPTER 16

The rhythm of the rain provided the perfect accompaniment to my dark mood. The tempo increased. I wrapped my blanket tighter around me. With the weather change came a much-appreciated coolness, although I held the fleece more for comfort than warmth.

I looked at the poster next to my bunk. *Great achievement is usually born of great sacrifice, and is never the result of selfishness.* I needed to get back on track here. Forget Ethan. Forget Chloe. The talent show loomed a few days away. Unfortunately, that meant working with all of Cabin Twelve's girls. I couldn't completely forget Chloe. *Great sacrifice.*

My teammates sat in their bunks. Julia had her long legs stretched out in front of her with a green elastic band wrapped around her feet. Her toes pointed up and down to a rhythm, possibly matching the one coming out of her earbuds. Niki sat in the bunk beneath her with big black headphones over her ears, flipping through a magazine.

Chloe's bed stood empty. The gloomy weather suited her character well. She had better be careful though. Witches and water? Not a good mix. She could melt out there.

Hannah hummed in the bunk below mine. I didn't recognize the tune, but the catchy melody drowned out the rain.

"Hannah?" I poked my head into her bunk.

She looked up from her journal. "Yeah?"

"What song is that?"

"Which one?"

"The one you're humming."

"Oh." Hannah flipped back a few pages in her journal. "Do you want to come and see?"

What better thing did I have to do? "Sure." I climbed down the ladder, bringing the blanket with me.

Hannah scooched over in her bunk, and I sat beside her.

"Here's the song." She pointed to the words as she sang.

"*You were always there for me, in the midst of everything. You were there. You were there. There were highs and there were lows, I didn't know where to go, but you found me and wouldn't let me fall.*"

Hannah's melodic voice filled the room.

"You wrote the lyrics?"

"Yeah."

"Who's the song for?"

"The words are about God." Her face glowed.

"God? If there's a God out there, he sure hasn't always been there for me." I dropped my eyes to the pattern on my blanket.

"Why do you say that?"

I looked back at Hannah and took a deep breath. "Let's just say my family will be a statistical divorce soon, and the drama's all my dad's fault."

Hannah touched the gold cross hanging around her neck. "I'm sorry, Geri. I know it probably doesn't help, but my dad messed up big time too. He left my family when I started kindergarten." Hannah's eyes shifted to the dark window. "His last day at home? I begged him to stay." She looked back at me. "But he didn't."

"Didn't that make you mad?"

"Sad at first and then, yeah, I stayed mad for a long time. When I got older, I realized I had to forgive him, more for myself than for him. The feelings ate me up inside."

"How did you forgive?"

"I prayed a lot, and I pleaded to God to help me. Finally, I gave him all my pain."

I squinted my eyes tight trying to envision the majestic being from the famous musical coming down to help Hannah. He got halfway there before the scene didn't make sense to me anymore. I popped open my eyes.

"I don't know a God like that."

Hannah squeezed my knee. "I hope you do someday."

The rain pounded louder on the roof.

"Can we pray for simpler stuff, like this rain to stop?"

Hannah's phone chimed with a text. She glanced at her cell. "Or ..."

She pushed past me and went over to Julia and Niki's bunk. "Julia. Niki." She tapped them both. Julia pulled out one earbud and Niki lifted her headphones.

"What?" Niki twisted to view our counselor.

"We're going outside." Hannah motioned to the door.

Julia pulled out her other earbud. "Isn't it still raining?"

"Yes." Hannah clapped her hands together. "That's the point. Camp Tradition. Late-night rain runs, and they don't happen every year. You girls are lucky!"

"Count me out." Julia went back to her stretches.

Niki took off her headphones and closed the magazine. "Going outside sounds better than looking at these phony people with perfect lives."

Hannah turned back toward me. "Geri?"

"Why not?" Rain runs stood as another camp tradition. Why stop having fun now?

After pulling on hooded sweatshirts and shoes, we headed out the door. I grabbed the blanket for good measure.

Hannah, Niki, and I stood on the porch as the rain pitter-pattered above us. We couldn't see much, but the few lamps along the dirt path revealed campers running and twirling in the rain.

"Whoo-hoo!" A group of guys ran past our cabin door. They wore nothing but shorts with no shoes. *Men.*

"Now what?" Niki scanned the sky.

Hannah ran down the stairs and out to the road. She lifted her hands and twirled around. "Just let go."

Niki shook her head. "I'm not putting my hair through that. Geri, you go."

"Not if you're not going."

"I have an excuse." Niki pointed to her hair covered in a decorative scarf.

I looked up at the roof keeping me dry then to Hannah running down the path. Should I?

"E-than! E-than! E-than!" I turned my head in the direction of his name, but the darkness covered the source.

Niki looked in the same direction. "You like him, don't you?"

I shook my head to end my daze. "What?"

"Ethan? You like him?"

The chanting grew closer.

I shrugged. "I guess."

Niki stepped further back under the porch. "I've known him for a while. He's a good guy. Give him a chance."

"But ..." I looked out into the rain.

"Yeah, I know. Chloe wants him, but what *doesn't* she want? She can't have it all." Niki turned the door handle but the *crescendo* shouting made her stop.

A group of guys became visible near the lamp in front of our cabin. Only something looked out of place. His feet danged in the air instead of being planted on the ground.

"E-than! E-than! E-than!"

The chanting made sense now. Ethan walked in a handstand down the road. When he neared the small path in front of our cabin, he turned toward me. The herd of guys paused on our front lawn.

Ethan stood. Cheers rang from the crowd before their attention turned to another one in the pack. "Ai-dan! Ai-dan! Ai-dan!" The lanky culprit flipped over and plopped upside down through the path's pooling puddles. The guys followed him, but Ethan stayed behind.

He brushed his soaking wet hair back, streams of raindrops still falling on his face. "What are you girls waiting for?"

"I've already had my fun." Niki pointed to her hair. "I'm going to protect this. You two go enjoy the moment."

Before she left, Niki put her hand on my shoulder. I had never seen her show physical compassion to anyone. The gesture made me feel like she tried to tell me something.

"All right, Geri. You look pretty dry under there. Time to join the fun." He put his hand out to me.

I stepped back. "I can't do this." Why did I keep pushing him away?

He stepped toward me. His wet T-shirt clung to his baseball muscles. "*This* as in the rain? Or *this* as in me?"

I looked at his clear blue eyes. "Maybe both." I adjusted the blanket around my shoulders. "I don't trust you."

His gaze dropped to his toes. "I've said all I could." He glanced back up at me. "Let me ask you this. Who do you trust?"

"I ..." The blanket stifled me, and I reached for my neck. "I don't know."

Ethan took a step backward. "Well, I hope you figure it out." He put his hands up. "I've done my part."

He backed up a bit more. "I'm going to go live life. You can stay under the roof—dry and safe." He turned and went down the stairs.

My heart pumped against my dry T-shirt as he walked away.

Flashbacks of my dad leaving came to mind. My fingers had pressed against the glass of the living room window as I watched him put the suitcase in the car, helpless, unable to change the unfolding scene.

I stepped to the edge of the porch and held on to the wooden post. Raindrops fell on my fingers. I refused to be a helpless kid anymore.

Ethan neared the lamppost. He turned his face toward our cabin before stepping out of its light and down the path.

No. Wait! Trusting Ethan could be *my* choice.

I threw off the blanket and started running, the rain hitting my face and the mud squishing beneath my shoes. I turned the corner and saw him plodding along the path.

"Ethan!"

He turned around and with all logic leaving my mind I ran myself right into his strong arms. I looked up at him. "I want to live life, too."

He smiled, drops of water trickling down his nose. "Good. Life's more fun this way." He held me tight, the rain washing away my insecurities.

Reasons I Don't Like Camp–
10. Late-night rain runs
Reasons I Like Camp–
4. Late-night rain runs with Ethan

CHAPTER 17

The large wooden beams on the cafeteria held the roof strong and steady like Ethan had held me last night. I had fallen asleep thinking of embraces in the rain, and in the morning the image clouded my mind once again. Hannah, Julia, and Niki chatted nearby but I didn't have the mental capacity to concentrate on their conversation.

"So." Abby plopped her tray next to mine. "*¿Qué pasó?*" What happened with you and Ethan last night?" Her eyes twinkled. How did she know anything happened? Did she have a secret video camera on our porch? The rain run lingered on my mind, and I usually told Abby everything, but I didn't have the energy to analyze the situation.

"How do you always know everything?"

"Late-night cabin runs are a whole camp tradition, and my cabin is next door to yours. I stopped to watch my best friend clinging to the cutest guy at camp. After Tyler."

I shook my head. "You're way too dramatic. We only—"

"Played out a romantic scene. I needed popcorn to watch the movie unfolding. You have a *novio*. You've never had a boyfriend before!"

"Would you stop announcing my dating history to the whole camp? Plus, he's not my boyfriend. We're just ..."

"Two people who hug in the rain?"

"Yes, precisely."

Abby squinted at me. "Yeah, that's a normal way to define a relationship."

I didn't know how to explain what had happened to Abby. I'm not sure I could explain the scene to myself. I knew one thing. Letting go of the porch post became one of the best decisions of my life.

Abby's hand flew in front of my face. "Earth to Geri."

I looked at her. "What?"

She pointed her fork at me. "See. Right there." She twirled the fork around in circles. "A lot going on in there."

"All right, you caught me. Maybe something is going on, but I'm not ready to dissect the situation until I have more info."

"Fair." Abby sipped her orange juice. "But you owe me details later. What about Chloe? Won't she be upset you're spending time with Ethan?"

"Do I care if she is?"

"Whoohoo, the real Geri's back!"

I couldn't help but laugh.

Hannah elbowed Abby. "What about you girls? What's your favorite part of camp?"

I gave Abby the death stare. But she ignored the hint.

"I know Geri's." She lifted her eyebrows.

Hannah turned to me. "Geri, do you have something to share?"

Julia and Niki looked at me.

"Nope." I shoved a grape in my mouth.

"A boyfriend isn't nothing." Abby winked.

I gave her the evil eye, but she kept smiling.

"You owe some of that to me, girl." Niki took a bite of a pancake. "You're welcome."

Hannah put down her glass. "Wait. What'd I miss?"

I slouched down to whisper. "Someone is going to hear you all, and he's not my boyfriend."

Hannah slouched down to match my level. "Who's not your boyfriend?"

"Ethan," I admitted to halt their gossip.

"What about Ethan?" Chloe's voice shot into my ear like a pesky fly at a picnic.

Abby grinned. "Oh, how last night Geri and Ethan—"

"Did nothing." I kicked Abby under the table. She scrunched her nose and gave me a dirty look.

I looked up at Chloe to see Bubble Gum, Nails, and Eyes standing next to her. Bubble Gum chewed while narrowing her eyes at us. Nails used one of her talons to pop a blueberry into her mouth, and Eyes blinked, her gold shimmer eyeshadow reflecting in the fluorescent light.

"Hmmm ..." Chloe pursed her glossy pink lips. "That's not what I heard."

Did everyone know my business?

Eyes batted her golden eyelids. "I saw something different."

In response, Bubble Gum popped her bubble, and Nails grabbed another fruit victim.

Niki turned around on the bench. "Oh quit, Chloe. It's not the girl's fault Ethan prefers her over the next Miss *Snotts*dale."

"I'll have you know Nicole ..." Chole folded her fingers over the right sleeve of her black sweater. "I now reside in Paradise Valley, a step up from a certain innercity neighborhood some people live in." Chloe darted her eyes toward Niki.

"You mean where you lived three families ago?" Niki smirked.

"I don't have to stay here and take this. C'mon, girls." Chloe snapped, and Gwen, Lynn, and Val followed, their perfectly wrapped ponytails swaying side to side as they paraded their wedges out the door.

"I wish you girls could all get along." Hannah sighed.

Niki swiveled back to the table. "I get along fine." She pointed to the door. "Talk to her."

"She's right." Julia motioned with her fork. "If we're going to have a presentable piece for the talent show, we need to work together."

Agreed.

"Geri." Abby tapped my arm. "Let me see your teeth."

I scrunched my eyebrows. "What? Why?"

"Just smile."

I sneered at Abby like Elgar after his dental surgery.

"No food but put the creepy grin away."

Strong hands lay on my shoulders. "Hey, you."

My heartbeat quickened, and I looked at Ethan. He showed a half-smile, revealing his adorable dimple. I ran my tongue across my teeth and silently thanked Abby for the heads up.

"Hey." I looked back at the table to see four pairs of eyes on us. I couldn't take the pressure. "Wanna take a walk or something?"

Niki raised her eyebrows at me. "Or something?" she mouthed. If she sat closer, I would have kicked her too.

"My thoughts exactly." Ethan squeezed my shoulders.

"Great." I looked back at the gawking eyes. "See you guys later."

"Don't forget teambuilding at nine." Hannah made that teacher-glare expression again.

I got up from the table. "Right. Teambuilding." Teambuilding and Chloe and bugs with their wings. These are a few of my favorite things.

I put my tray on the conveyor belt and followed Ethan out the door. He had on green shorts and a white V-neck. The sleeves of the tee strained against his biceps. I would stay in those arms forever.

Another sunny day greeted us. The midmorning heat hadn't set in yet to taunt my sweat glands. Ethan took my hand, and our fingers laced together. I never wanted the moment to end.

Ethan squeezed my hand. "I've been thinking."

I didn't respond and waited to hear what magical thing he had to say.

Ethan cleared his throat. "Would you be OK with me helping Chloe?"

Magic over. I wanted the moment to end.

"What do you mean?" I rubbed the back of my neck. Despite the morning coolness, I began to feel clammy.

Ethan swayed our hands back and forth as we walked. "Before you and I were ... um, before I knew you, and Chloe and I were ... when Chloe and I used to hang out a lot, I helped her practice her vocals with the guitar." He ran his free hand through his hair. "She asked me if I'd help her out. She doesn't know many people here who play guitar."

Doesn't know many people who play guitar my rear end. More like she couldn't wait to get her tentacles on him.

"Aren't you afraid she's going to attack you again?"

Ethan squeezed my hand. "We cleared that up. Agreed we're just friends."

Just friends. Right. Were we talking about the same Chloe? Tall. Blonde. Hates puppies?

Ethan looked at me with wide eyes. My mouth remained glued shut. What could I say?

I heard wheels on the dirt behind us. A voice shouted, "Beep! Beep!"

Ethan grabbed my waist and moved me out of the biker's way. I put my arms around his neck and looked into his honest eyes. He laced his fingers behind my back and pulled me closer. He smelled like Dove soap and sandalwood.

"What do you say? Are you OK with us working together?"

I tumbled deep into his sparkling blue eyes. I gave in. "Yeah."

He pulled me close with his strong arms and embraced me. "You're the best."

The best at what? Falling for you. Definitely. Being fine with you helping out Ms. De Vil? Chances are as good as her taking a liking to Dalmatians.

CHAPTER 18

No need to run from Cruella anymore. I had practically given her the skin off my back as she held my hand at the edge of a small forest. Blindfolded.

"Ready, girls?" Our counselor's chipper voice interrupted my nightmare.

Hannah could be happy. She had blindfold-less life to live.

"You're going to have to work together to walk through the forest. Chloe and Julia, you'll need to give clear directions. Geri and Niki, you'll need to trust them." Trust her to do what? Lead me to her evil mansion? No thanks.

Julia's accent rang loud and clear. "Don't worry, Nicole. I will give pristine directions."

I only heard gum-smacking from my tour guide.

"And go!' Hannah shouted the command with enthusiasm.

Chloe's cold hand pulled mine, and I lurched forward. "Let's go."

I stumbled and my hands caught the forest floor. "Nice one, Chloe." I stood up and brushed the dirt off my hands. "We're supposed to be working as a team." I'm already letting you work with Ethan.

"You're the clumsy one, Geraldine." The blindfold blocked the fire I tried to shoot out of my eyes.

Chloe's hand pushed my back. "Keep walking."

I took a hesitant step determined not to fall into the dirt again. With Chloe as my partner, I'd rather navigate the woods alone. At least then, I wouldn't be frightened for my life.

"Great. We should finish by Christmas at this rate," Chloe said.

I stuck my foot out and moved another step forward. "You're not helping any."

Chloe's voice seemed extra cold. "Why should I help you? You don't seem to need any help getting what you want."

"What are you talking about?" Branches scraped against my leg as I stumbled through the forest. Ouch. "You know, you could help a girl out here."

"Like you helped me with Ethan? I don't think so."

She couldn't pin their break-up on me, especially since I signed off on their practice sessions. I took another step and tripped again. I gave up and sat down.

"You know, I could have got him back without you in the picture." Her voice hovered over me.

"This has nothing to do with me."

"So, I'm the problem."

I took a deep breath. "No Chloe. I'm sure there's a rich ... good looking ... cat-loving guy out there for you."

"Cat loving? Who said I love cats?"

A stick poked my leg when I shifted my weight. I gripped the twig and drew circles in the dirt. "Are you going to help through this maze or what?" When she didn't answer, I threw the stick and crossed my arms. "Because if I fall one more time and break a finger, I can't play next week. Say goodbye to our piece for the talent show."

Her shoe shuffled against the dirt. "You're pretty confident we couldn't replace you. There are loads of pianists at camp."

I laid my head on my knees. Mozart, Beethoven, Bach.

Chloe's cool hand took mine, and she helped me stand. "I don't want to risk my chances. I've got a lot riding on the performance. There's a stump to your right. Turn left."

I followed her directions and took a more confident step, letting go of her hand. Chloe continued to give me instructions, and we made progress. At least my backend stayed off the ground.

"Are you trying to kill me?" Niki's voice met us further in the forest.

"Of course not!" Julia's tone rose an octave higher.

"Then why didn't you tell me?"

The fighting. The battle. Niki and Julia's song played in my head.

"I did. I said—" Mozart's *Rondo Alla Turca*.

"You did not." Niki's new piece.

"I did too." Mozart.

"Geraldine, stop. Take my hand."

Chloe's dainty hand took mine, and I envisioned her leading me through the forest. Two opposites coming together to work as a team. Like Niki and Julia. Maybe we could extend the teamwork to the stage.

"I have an idea."

"Two steps to the right. For the group?"

I followed her directions. "No, for the raccoons in this forest." After she didn't say anything, I continued. "Yes, for our group."

"Duck."

I dipped my head, wondering if an object blocked my way or if Chloe made me look like a fool on purpose. She still held my hand, confirming the need to crouch. Voluntary physical contact seemed too drastic for a joke.

"Will the plan help our performance?"

Our? I'm sure Chloe meant herself.

"No, I want to make our piece the worst one in the whole show."

"Very funny. Three steps to the right. Let's hear the idea after we're done."

The rest of our journey dragged on forever. When we finally finished, I ripped off the blindfold and ran to our counselor.

She clapped. "Wow. Geri, Chloe. I'm impressed. You made good time."

"Hannah." I rested my hands on my knees to catch my breath. Then I pointed to her. "Your song."

"What song?" Hannah frowned.

"The song you were humming last night in the cabin. The chorus is about people, or you said God, but the words could be about people, coming together."

"Go on ..." Hannah scrunched her eyebrows.

"After Niki and Julia do the fighting scene, they mesh their parts together and dance to your song."

Hannah smiled. "Geri, ending with a duet is a fantastic idea. What do you think, Chloe?" Chloe had joined us in her wedges. Wedges take about twice as long as sneakers to get anywhere.

"Who will sing?" Chloe put her hands on her hips.

"You will." I pointed to her.

Chloe popped her gum. "I need to hear the melody first, of course. Make sure the notes will showcase my voice. And if the song does ..." She turned in the direction of Niki and Julia's fighting. "Then the plan could work."

Wow. First, she leads me safely through a forest and now she likes my idea. Maybe she'll open a dog shelter next.

"You are seriously the worst leader ever." Niki appeared behind the trees at the edge of the clearing.

"To be a leader, you must have followers who are willing to listen." Julia's tall frame stepped out of the forest.

"I would if listening got me anywhere." Niki ripped off her blindfold.

Hannah put her hands on me and Chloe's shoulders. "I'm glad the fighting part of the piece will be authentic." She squeezed our shoulders before letting go. "But we still have to work on the coming together part."

Reasons I Like Camp–

5. *Not dying in the forest with Chloe.*
6. *Authentic dance fighting*

CHAPTER 19

You know when you've been mad at someone for eons and then you make up, but your brain is still confused because the "I don't like them" path is worn down? Welcome to my feelings about Chloe.

"Geri, I love this idea!" Hannah dug under the bottom bunk to reveal her journal.

"Remember, I said I need to make sure the vocals fit my voice before I commit." Chloe inspected her nails. They'd reached a ridiculous length for camp but were perfect for poking puppies. Whoops. The snide thoughts seemed to generate on autopilot.

"Here's the song." Hannah pulled out the journal and flipped through the pages. She stood next to Chloe and pointed. "I'll show you how the melody goes."

Hannah's beautiful voice filled the cabin, and Chloe smiled. If Cruella smiles at things other than gaining fur coats. Be nice, Geri. Be nice.

Hannah finished and looked at Cru—, I mean Chloe.

Chloe pursed her bubble gum pink lips together. "The song will do."

"Great!" Hannah had an amazing ability to be positive about Chloe's rude comments.

"Do you have music for the melody, Hannah?" I peeked at her journal.

Hannah turned the page. "Ummm, no. Sorry. I sing the song from memory."

"No worries." I grabbed my tote bag with the staff paper from Tyler. "I'll go to the studio and write a melody to match."

"Good idea, Geri. You're so talented." Hannah ripped the page out of her journal and handed me the song. "Chloe, you should go with her to write a tune to match your voice. I'll stay here and practice with Julia and Niki."

I gave Chloe my best I'm-trying-to-be-genuine smile. I did need her to come with me, but that meant I'd be spending actual time with her. Although with the song, we'd be spending lots of time together. Why did I devise this plan again? Oh yeah, because the whole ordeal would make our piece look good, improving my chances of getting the scholarship.

Chloe straightened her fuchsia top. "Let's go, then."

Hannah squeezed my shoulder. "I'm glad the song helps."

"Me too. Thanks, Hannah." I dropped an extra pencil in my tote bag.

Chloe and I left, walking to the music studio. The path seemed longer next to someone who used to be my arch enemy. I would have walked faster, but I had to slow myself down to keep the pace of Chloe's plodding wedges.

"The vocal suits me." Chloe pointed to the paper I had in my hand.

The statement lingered as either an attempt to be nice or have a normal conversation. Very well, I could try talking to her.

"Yeah, I heard the song last night. The melody is great."

Awkward pause. Birds tweeting.

"Did you do the rain run last night?" I tried to keep the "conversation" going.

"No, I can't get wet."

Oh right, she'd melt. Oops—Mean Geri again. I mean she'd ... blossom too much, like a flower long overdue.

What did I just try to be? A poet?

"I mean I didn't want to get wet." Chloe corrected herself.

I imagined Chloe running in the rain in her wedges. Bam! Girl down.

"I don't like to get wet either." My response added to the awkwardness of the conversation. Oh, your favorite color is blue and you love baby chicks too. Awesome. Let's wear navy and go to the petting zoo sometime.

"So, you didn't go?" Chloe broke my thoughts.

"Didn't go where?"

"The rain run, duh?"

Does running to catch Ethan in the rain count as going?

"I ..." Oh no, could I escape talking about last night? I regretted bringing up the subject in the first place. Chloe and I had reached an awkward level of stability. I couldn't mention the "E" word and cause everything to come tumbling down.

"A friend made me go." I hoped she would be satisfied.

Chloe nodded. "Ethan." It came out more of a statement.

"He made you go before too?" The question popped out before I realized the awkwardness of asking your ex-arch enemy about her ex-boyfriend.

Chloe sped up in her peep-toe wedges. A little too much. She tripped and landed with a gigantic thud on the rocky path before anyone could say "Dalmatian."

Wedges aren't made for camp.

I stuck my hand out to help her up, but she stood on her own. She brushed the back of her white shorts. White shorts aren't made for camp either.

Then she glared at me. "No, I went after him. I can embarrass myself more than once, Geraldine." Seeming to be satisfied with her shorts, (I wouldn't tell her what they looked like from the back), she started walking on the path again.

I followed her. "It's not embarrassing to go after what you want." Pouncing when the other girl who likes the guy is right around the corner is heartless, however.

Chloe shook her head. "When he's already turned you down once, it is. But let's forget guys. We need to work on this piece."

Happy to move on from the subject I had accidentally started, I let out a deep breath. We walked the remaining short distance to the music studio in silence. I distracted myself by keeping my eyes on the lyrics in my hand, trying to remember the melody.

When we reached the entrance, I led Chloe down the hall to Tyler's office. I tried to knock loud enough to be heard over the music blasting from his earbuds. When pounding on the door didn't work, I tapped him on the shoulder.

He turned around. "Hey there, Geri." He looked at Chloe. "New friend?" His question held tremendous depth.

"This is Chloe, one of my cabinmates." Chloe put up a hand and waved her fingers.

Tyler stood. "Hey, Chloe, nice to meet one of Geri's friends." I cringed at the chummy word.

"Is there a room open? We need to write more music." I held up the paper in my hand.

"More music? Adventurous." Tyler checked a clipboard lying on his desk. "Room two is open."

"Great, thanks," I charged out the door desperate to get the whole ordeal over with.

We walked to the open practice room. I sat on the piano bench, and Chloe pulled a chair over from the corner.

"Do you remember the melody?" I put the paper and pencil on the piano's music stand.

"Of course." She tightened her ponytail.

I handed her Hannah's song. "Sing the first verse, and I'll try to match the notes."

Chloe cleared her throat. "All right."

I put my fingers on the keys and waited. And waited. And waited. "At this rate, we'll be done by Christmas." I hoped mocking her wouldn't ruin our new non-hating relationship.

Chloe let out a deep breath. "I can't sing with you staring at me."

"I'm looking at the piano."

"You know what I mean."

"And you're supposed to perform in front of the whole camp?"

Chloe threw her hands in the air, and Hannah's song floated to the floor. "I hate singing in front of people, but I have to. I'm aging out of the system in three years. My only chance of going to college is winning the scholarship."

Cruella entered the scholarship competition and admitted her foster care status? My brain couldn't compute all the information. I hoped she didn't shine at singing as well as she made fur coats.

I tried to push my eyeballs back in my head and compose myself. "I get it. I'm entering the scholarship too." I zoned in on the piano keys to block her out. I'll get you, my pretty, and your little wedges too.

I knew one thing for sure. We needed to get the song done for either one of us to have a chance at winning."Why don't you look the other way then?"

Out of the corner of my eye, I saw Chloe get up, grab the paper, and walk toward the window. She placed her long fingernails on the window ledge and peered outside. "Ready?"

My fingers bent at the keys. "Ready."

That is when I heard the worst thing on the Camp Hi-Lu-Ma-Po planet. The voice of an angel flowed out of my enemy.

CHAPTER 20

Putting on my one-piece bathing suit felt like stuffing an air mattress back in its box. Another reason I hated camp. The activities made you uncomfortable in mind, spirit, and shoulders.

The cool water reached my ankles and felt good on my feet after another hot July day. And after my heart attack following Chloe's vocal practice ... or should I say Ursula post Ariel's voice?

The opposite of feeling good? The impending volleyball game ... in a lake ... in a sausage one-piece bathing suit.

The net stood large and looming, begging me not to humiliate myself. Athletic humiliation proved to be inevitable my volleyball friend.

A few of my teammates chatted on the grass before the "traditional" Camp Hi-Lu-Ma-Po volleyball match because according to the High School Handbook every teen experience must include an embarrassing sports moment. Don't ask me why. However, *one* good thing came out of the game.

"Geri!"

Ethan. We played in the same match. And I do have to say, the muscular scene before me trumped the uncomfortableness of the sausage suit. Although unfair, the rules banned bikinis or two pieces for the girls, while guys got to wear normal swimming trunks at camp. Also thankful for that. Ethan's athleticism appeared fully visible, and I wasn't complaining.

He came closer. His mouth moved, but I had no idea what he said. My senses narrowed to my vision. Of his abs. "Ready for the volleyball tournament?" He stood in front of me with his baseball ... everything. Major heart palpitation moment.

"We are so ready!" Abby appeared next to me, her sky blue swimsuit complementing her olive skin tone. "Our cabins are going to cream your cabins."

Ethan crossed his arms over his broad chest. "You are?"

Abby pulled a pair of sunglasses down from her head. "Definitely."

"Campers, take your places," Hannah shouted from the nearby grass.

Niki, Julia, and the other girls from Abby's cabin joined us in the lake. Chloe sat on her towel throne in the grass while her posse tinkered on their phones beneath wide-brimmed hats. Bubble Gum popped her gum before giggling at something on the screen. Eyes inspected her cell from underneath oversize sunglasses while Nails' neon-orange thumbs typed five words per second.

Ethan looked up at the phone fest on the grass. "Good luck." He turned and ran to the other side of the net. My eyes couldn't help but follow.

Water splashed me. "Geri, you're going to need to watch the ball during the game."

I looked at Abby. "I know."

"Your eyes seemed pretty fixed on something else."

"Don't worry. I'll pay attention."

"To what, I'm not sure." Abby nodded toward Ethan.

I shook my head and walked backward to take the position next to her in the back non-serving corner. Julia stood in front of me, and Niki took the spiking position. Abby's two cabin mates settled in the last two spots.

"Hey there, Geri." Surfer Tyler appeared in the water with a whistle around his neck. He ran past us to stand next to the net.

"Tyler." Abby waved so hard I thought her hand might fall off. Now who needed to be reminded to watch the ball?

The game got off to a rough start. Abby's teammate, Kaitlyn, served first. She hit the ball into the net, and the point went to the guys' side. 0-1. The guys' starter targeted Kaitlyn again. And again. And again. 0-6.

On the next serve, Abby dove in front of Kaitlyn and made contact. Two guys crashed into each other unable to salvage the play. They argued before tossing the ball to Abby's other cabin mate, Sydney. 1-6.

Sydney threw the ball in the air a few times before serving. She jumped and hit the target but missed the ground beneath her. Water splashed beside her when she fell.

Tyler blew his whistle and ran over to her. "Need a hand?"

Abby ran to Tyler's side. "*¿Estás bien?* You OK, Syd?"

"Yeah. Just trying to wipe those smirks off the boys' faces." She stood.

Tyler rubbed the back of his neck. "Touché."

Abby stared at Tyler too long to qualify for a normal conversational pause. I cleared my throat loud enough for my mother to hear back in Phoenix.

Abby shook her head and came back to earth. She turned to Sydney. "You should sit this one out."

"Then they'll really win." Sydney limped back toward her corner.

"Sydney, I can't let you play injured." He pointed to Chloe lounging in the grass. "Cabin Twelve's sub will come in." We do have a sub. One who would sink the game.

Abby crouched down next to Sydney and put her hand out. "*Ven*. C'mon, Chloe's going to take your place." Sydney gave in and let Abby help her to the grass.

Tyler blew his whistle and shouted. "Sub in for the girls." Chloe didn't move.

He looked at me. "Someone needs to get Chloe."

Did he mean me? When no one else moved, I began my walk to the queen's throne. "This will go over well," I hissed under my breath.

"Chloe." I tapped my foot on the grass.

She lay on the towel with one ankle dangling over her knee. Super invested in the game on her cell phone.

"Chloe." I folded my arms over my chest.

She scrolled her phone. "I heard you. I'm busy."

I tried to summon the nice Geri. "We need you in the game."

She didn't look up from her phone. "I'm hanging with the girls. Plus, I don't get wet."

I turned my attention to Bubble Gum, Nails, and Eyes. They knew how to spend good quality time, not looking at each other and all.

"Sydney's out. We need you, or we have to forfeit."

"So, forfeit. Why are we playing volleyball when we all care more about music?"

"Teambuilding ... woman empowerment ... camp rite of passage ..."

Her dangling foot continued its rhythm. "You're really selling the game."

I turned around to see both volleyball teams peering at me. I looked at Ethan in particular and raised my shoulders. He came over.

"Chloe." Her foot on top of her knee fidgeted. "Yes, Ethan?"

"Get in the game, or I'm going to tell everyone what I found in your bag last summer."

Chloe's eyes darted to him. "You wouldn't dare."

He walked backward. "Try me." He pointed to her. "Get your hiney up."

Chloe took a deep breath and stood. "Fine."

She threw her phone on her towel. Eyes looked up a second before turning back to her screen. Bubble Gum and Nails didn't flinch.

"But I'm not playing. I'll stand there and get a tan." Chloe pulled at the sleeve of her sweater, but then stopped. "Or just stand there," she said more to herself.

Chloe stomped toward the lake and took the serving position in front of Niki. Niki backed up, encroaching on Chloe's space. Good call.

On the guys' turn, Niki squatted with her hands out. She hit the ball like women swatted away Beethoven, and her target splashed into the water. We cheered. 2–8.

She served an ace twice. 4–8. By the fourth time, the guys must have caught on because they hit the ball back to us. Julia's height dominated the net. She scored in bounds. 5–8.

Niki prepared for her fifth serve. One of the guys volleyed the ball toward an oblivious Chloe. The white missile flew into Chloe's side, projecting her into the lake.

Ursula exploded.

"I told you I don't get wet!" Chloe slapped her hands in the shallow water.

A second later, she screamed while dancing around the lake. "What is crawling on me?" She turned in circles. "Get the bug out of my sweater!" She pulled off her black shield and a leaf fell to the water.

With her arms bare, I could see her full scar. The pink speckled oval circled between her wrist and elbow. A rim of healed skin stood out against the tint of her natural complexion.

Chloe looked horrified and scooped up the sweater, pressing the masquerade into the wound. "I'm done." She marched to the grass and threw her towel over her shoulder. Her entourage followed suit.

As she walked the sleeve of the black bandage swayed from side to side. One more bump and the cover-up would fall to the ground, leaving her exposed for the world to see. Did this fractured angel need the scholarship more than me?

Reasons I Don't Like Camp–

11. Volleyball matches

Reasons I Like Camp–

7. Ethan in a swimsuit

CHAPTER 21

The piano stand held three pieces: Niki's original, Hannah's piece, and Mozart's sonata. I needed to combine them like Mendelssohn blended notes.

I heard a knock at the door. "Hey, Beautiful." Ethan's tall frame appeared in the doorway.

Did someone that good looking call me beautiful? I must have been in my own fairy tale. Cue the singing birds.

Ethan put his hands on my shoulders. "What are you working on?"

I placed blank staff paper on the piano. "Trying to merge these three pieces into something promising for the talent show."

Ethan massaged my shoulders with his thumbs. My stomach fluttered.

"You'll find the right balance. Are you going to lunch? We could walk together."

"Yeah, in a bit." I straightened the papers.

"Come get me when you're ready. I'll be practicing down the hall." He smiled, revealing his dimple.

I tucked my hair behind my ears. "Sounds good."

After he left, I sat in a daze for a few seconds before the notes on the sheet music became clear again. What did I need to do again? Oh yeah, save our piece for the talent show. Win the scholarship. Get to Juilliard.

I worked for a while and the melodies came together. A little *allegro* for Niki here. A little *legato* for Julia there.

A full page stared back at me. My eyes wandered to the window and my thoughts floated to Ethan. That much gorgeous sat nearby, and I hid in a practice room? Time to put the *coda* on this practice session.

"I can afford a ten-minute break," I said aloud to the empty room. I set the timer on my phone for good measure and made my way down the hall.

Every door stood open except two. Eenie meenie miney mo. I pick you, and here we go.

I turned the knob sorting through excuses if I entered the wrong room, but no need. I opened the door to my prince charming.

Ethan sat on the piano bench with his guitar. "Couldn't wait to see me, huh?" He raised his eyebrows.

How did he know? I bit my bottom lip. Are people supposed to admit a need for accompaniment?

"I've been playing around with Broadway songs." He shifted through a pile of sheet music on the floor and chose one. "Here's a song from Phantom. There's a piano part. Are you in?"

Did he even need to ask? I grabbed the music out of his hands. "I'm always up for Phantom."

"Note taken." Ethan changed his seat from the piano bench to a chair in the corner. Less appealing, but whatever.

I sat on the Ethan-less bench and put my phone on top of the piano. A refreshing completed piece of sheet music stared back at me. The title reflected a popular Broadway love song.

I stretched my fingers onto the opening chords. The blend of notes resounded in the room.

The melody continued as I played, and soon Ethan entered with the guitar. Since I'd never tackled the piece before, I had to keep my eyes on the music, but I desperately wanted to look at Ethan. The chorus repeated, and I allowed my eyes to roam.

His eyes met mine, and instead of turning back to the music, I continued to get lost in the quiet calm of his gaze. My fingers replayed the same melody, E-D-E-F, unable to convince my brain to turn back to the black and white notes.

Ethan stood and continued to strum on the guitar. He sang the first line of the familiar song, still looking at me.

My fingers repeated the E-D-E-F melody one last time, and my brain fogged. He stopped right in front of me, and my hands went limp on the keys. Ethan continued to hum and play as he bent over. I closed my eyes, unable to turn back now, and felt the touch of his soft lips.

My heart hammered against my chest like a cardiac drum set. Ethan pressed his forehead against mine, humming and lingering for a moment before kissing me one more time. I opened my eyes, and my smile met his.

Best. Break. Ever.

My cheeks burned, and I turned back to the sheet music trying to find my spot, but still immersed in the kiss. My eyes scanned the notes, but the effort didn't matter. Everything in my brain turned mushy, the memory of Ethan's lips controlling every thought.

The melody of my phone alarm sounded. Ten minutes ended. And my ability to control my cognitive processing.

"I'd better get back to practicing." And I needed to get out of there before I lost all rationale. I stood and turned to Ethan. My cheeks felt warm again.

"Right. I've stolen too much of your practice time already." Ethan stopped playing and squeezed my hand as I walked by. "I'll see you in a few for lunch." The warmth went from my fingers, up to my arm, and settled in my heart.

I floated back to my practice room, humming the magical song and waltzing side to side down the hall. Seeing the slew of music on the piano stand helped me come back to earth. "Hello Flagstaff, Arizona," I said aloud and closed the door. "I'm here to work." My fingers touched the keys, but a fog clouded my brain.

I started at the top of the music and made my way through the first page. A knock sounded at the door. Could Ethan not wait to see me either?

"Come on in," I shouted expecting to return to Dreamland. Tyler's surfer hair appeared in the doorway. Or Maui.

"Oh, hey." I shifted on the bench.

"Need any help?"

Loaded question. Oh, he meant the piece. I looked at my in-progress composition. The music needed to be perfect, and Tyler had the expertise. Plus, my brain needed help to function properly after the moment with Ethan. "Will you listen to the harmony and give me your opinion?"

"Sure thing." Tyler pointed to the piano bench. "I moved the extra chair to another room. Mind if I sit?"

I scooched over, and Tyler sat next to me. Our composition filled the room while I played. I finished and looked at him, my hands still on the keys.

He nodded. "Sounds good, but what if at this part—" He pointed to one of the lines of music and placed his other hand on the piano next to mine. "—You made the notes an octave higher?" He began playing. The high register of the notes added a missing intensity.

The door opened without a knock. "Geri, are you—" Ethan put his hands in his pockets. "What's going on?"

I took my hands off the keys and shifted on the bench. "Tyler's helping me compose our piece."

"She doesn't need much help, man. She's good." Tyler patted my back.

Ethan took a step backward. "I know, *man*. I'll let you guys get back to work."

"Ethan!" His expression freaked me.

He closed the door.

"Cool dude." Tyler smiled and played another two bars. "I'm off in fifteen. We better get crack-a-lackin' if we're going to finish this."

Tyler must live in a world of surfboards and piano keys because he seemed oblivious to the obvious.

The front door of the music studio slammed shut. I sprung from the bench and hit my leg on the piano. Ouch. "Can we finish the piece tomorrow?"

Tyler added a few eighth notes to the sheet music "Got tomorrow off. Besides, I'm feeling the inspiration now. We can finish before lunch if we power through."

"I'll be right back then." I half-ran down the hall, limping from the pain in my thigh. When I opened the front door, I froze. Ethan had already reached the main path. And not on his own.

I would know her ponytail anywhere.

The curl of Chloe's hair swayed from side to side. Did she have an Ethan tracker in her black sweater?

Air filled deep in my chest to call out his name. No. I held my breath for a few seconds before releasing the thought into the muggy atmosphere. Warmth developed around the outside of my eyes. I leaned back against the open door.

From inside I heard a slight *crescendo* of my piece. I wiped a tear from my eye and stepped back inside the music studio, softly closing the front door. Why did I have to get so upset? Walking with someone doesn't signal the start of a relationship unless the stroll is down the aisle.

People walk all the time. I helped an elderly man across the street last week, and I didn't end up dating him. Deception is annoying when your brain tricks you into thinking small things are big deals.

Amid the romantic rollercoaster, my true mission remained clear. I needed to win the scholarship.

I walked back into the practice room to see Tyler jamming out with the perfect blend of *adagio* and *allegro*. His head moved back and forth to match the beat as his fingers leaped off the keys.

Out the window, Ethan and Chloe disappeared down the path. I turned from them to the piano. I had come to camp to play music. I could straighten things out later.

Tyler finished playing with a few dramatic chords. I turned my finger in a circle and pointed to the sheet music. "Teach me *that*." I walked back to the piano bench and sat down.

Thoughts of Ethan lingered in the pit of my stomach, but I *decrescendo*ed the distraction until the feelings turned into a mere grace note, barely visible.

Ethan had kissed me, five minutes ago. Kissing qualified as a big deal. Walking? Not a big deal. Ants walk, and they're not a big deal. Unless they're in my cabin.

Winning the scholarship. Also a big deal. Once again, I immersed myself in the music, but this time a melody played in the background.

E-D-E-F.
Then some bass clef.
Listen to me later.
Please don't date her.
That's all I ask of you.

CHAPTER 22

Swat! The bug spray seemed to be made out of candy instead of whatever repelling agents it supposedly had. At least I got the little guy. I flicked the dead mosquito off my arm.

The sun curved behind the camp stage, spilling an orange glow over the camp benches. Dusk brought relief from the heat, but the mixture of sweat and sunscreen still covered my skin.

Abby and I sat waiting for the singing competition to start. The platform in front of us stood empty except for a few speakers and a microphone, all you needed for a camp sing-along.

Apparently, the show signified another camp tradition. Anyone could enter, but Hannah told me the voice students used the show to practice their "stage presence" before the official camp performance.

"Who do you think will win?" Abby grabbed my arm.

"I don't know many of the people."

"Chloe entered. You know her."

I leaned my chin on my hand. "Don't remind me."

"I thought you two were getting along."

"More like not killing each other."

Abby rolled her eyes. "You're being such a drama queen. I saw you guys walking to the music studio the other day. You didn't look like arch enemies to me."

"We have to be civil if we want a chance to shine at the talent show. Remember the motto? Perform to Shine." I showed Abby my best spirit fingers.

Abby turned and pointed to my yellow Camp Hi-Lu-Ma-Po T-shirt. "Yes, and you will. I know you have a heart in there somewhere, Tin Man. Are you telling me you're only being nice to Chloe for some talent show?"

I put my hands on the log bench and turned toward her. "*Some* talent show? Abby, this is my life we're talking about. The talent show is going to give me a chance at a scholarship."

Abby turned back to face the stage. "There's more to life than winning, Geri."

I knew she had a point, but I considered Juilliard my *dream*. If I didn't have a time slot at Carnegie Hall, what did I have? Messed up parents and wasted practice hours?

Chloe walked down the first row reserved for the performers. Her ponytail swung like a metronome before settling on her black sweater when she took a seat.

Next, Ethan appeared carrying his guitar, the same guitar he held a few hours ago when he kissed me. Ethan? I didn't know he entered the competition. A brunette sitting next to Chloe moved over and he sat next to her.

Then my brain started freaking out.

I hit Abby's leg and she yelped. "¡Ay! What?"

I nodded in the direction of the unfortunate pair. "I didn't know Ethan planned on singing tonight."

Abby followed my gaze. "Oh, he's probably accompanying Chloe. That's what he used to do when they—" She stopped herself and looked away.

"—When they dated." I finished for her, scratching at invisible mosquito bites. "I know. He told me."

Major brain freak out.

Abby took my frantically scratching hands. "Geri." When I didn't look at her, she said my name again. "GERI!"

That time I looked. "What?"

Abby looked me straight in the eyes. "Take a deep breath."

I let my chest fill with the muggy air. Hopefully, I hadn't let any mosquitos in.

Abby's eyes did not leave mine. "Now repeat after me. Ethan is not my father."

"Ethan is not my father."

"Chloe and Ethan are just friends."

"Chloe and Ethan are just friends."

"Friends do nice things for each other."

"Friends do nice things for each other."

My heartbeat slowed in my chest from *presto* to *allegro* to *allegretto*, which didn't qualify as healthy, but manageable.

Abby let go of my hands. "You could take pointers from him." She nudged me with her elbow. "You know, start doing nice things for me." She smiled.

"What do you call coming here?" I spread my arms out wide.

"Your window of opportunity." She looked back toward Chloe and Ethan. "And for more than music." Abby lifted her eyebrows up and down.

I looked at Ethan and sighed.

"What aren't you telling me?" She hissed the command in my ear.

I remembered Ethan kissing me a few hours ago. I shook my head. "I don't know what you're talking about."

Abby's eyes widened, and she put both hands on my shoulders. "Spill."

In fear of my life, I relented. "We kinda sorta kissed."

She opened her mouth wide enough to inhale Chloe. And her ponytail. "You-He-What?" She squeezed my arm like Beethoven grinding his morning coffee beans and shrieked. Nearby campers turned to look at us.

I tried to undo her grip. " Shush. You're making a scene."

She clasped her hands in front of her heart. "This is the best news EVER." She moved her eyes to the sky. "Ethan and Geri *por siempre*." She sighed. Then she turned to me. "Please put in a good word for me with Tyler?"

I rolled my eyes. "No, and whatever we are won't be forever if you-know-who gets back in."

"Geri, you're going to have to start trusting him."

"It's not him I don't trust." I muttered my response under my breath but Abby's expression told me she heard me loud and clear.

"Good evening, campers!" Maury stepped on stage. "Welcome to our annual sing-along."

"They should make a program with all their annual events for campers to keep track of them all." I leaned forward and propped my head up with my fist.

Abby knocked my knee with hers.

"Owww." I scooched further down the bench.

She stared straight ahead.

"Tonight's competition is a fun way to prepare our singers for their big day on the stage. Many of our musicians have a buddy on stage with them, their instrument." Maury laughed to himself and his belly jiggled. The audience remained silent. "But our singers only have themselves and their voices." He tapped the microphone and a screech bellowed from the speaker. Several campers in front of us covered their ears.

Maury chuckled again. "Sorry about that. Sit back, relax, and welcome our first singer." He clapped as he walked off stage and several campers joined in the applause.

The girl nearest the stage stood and walked to the microphone. Her long black hair draped over her white blouse and reached to her waist. She smoothed the sides of her lilac skirt before standing still. A few seconds later, a familiar tune came from the speakers. Several campers sang along with her. Her tone stayed on key but didn't sound extraordinary. Definitely not a threat.

A boy with red sneakers walked on stage next. He lowered the mic and stepped behind the stand. When the beat started, he exploded with a rap song. The stage became his microwave and his voice burst like a bag of instant popcorn. He sent word kernels popping everywhere.

"Go, Leo," a couple of girls chanted. Probably his young admirers. The moment seemed like the perfect opportunity for a mic drop, but he resisted.

Next up. Chloe and Ethan. Their names together burned my ears. Abby squeezed my shoulder. "Just friends remember."

Just friends I said in my head. *Just friends.*

"Yay, Ethan!" A shout rang from the crowd. Chloe's wedges pounded across the stage as she took her place. Ethan smiled and stopped a couple of feet from her. She pulled at the sleeves of her sweater and nodded toward him. He strummed his guitar and bobbed to the beat.

While he played, Chloe took a step back from the front of the stage and bowed her head. Did she need to get in the zone? Breathe? Pray? After an eight-count, she stepped forward, snapped open her ice-blue eyes, and grabbed the microphone.

Her tone during the first line sounded strong and determined. And remarkable.

She reached out to the audience with her free hand. She didn't look like the nervous girl I'd seen in the practice room. Almost everyone in the camp clapped along with the music. The almost could be traced to my frozen stance.

I looked at Abby who had joined in.

Abby shrugged. "I'm sorry, but she's good."

Chloe reached the chorus and stepped further out on the stage. Ethan smiled and took a few steps back. As she sang, she moved across the platform and gestured to the audience. Cheers rang from the campers. Major style points.

After the bridge, Chloe let go. Her angelic voice rang past the tall pine trees and the entire camp leaped to their feet. Almost the entire camp. My feet pressed onto the ground. She couldn't headline as Whitney, but she performed well. Great actually.

My scholarship chances plummeted.

Chloe finished and applause filled the clearing in the forest. I looked at Abby smiling and clapping. She'd won over my best friend. I needed a miracle to win the scholarship.

Reasons I Don't Like Camp–
12. Chloe's voice

CHAPTER 23

My pencil tapped the piano as I scoured the music. Could the melody be better anywhere? I'd already practiced the song a dozen times. The notes felt natural on my fingers, but I needed the composition to be the best.

I wished Ethan could listen and tell me if the song qualified as scholarship-worthy. He would be honest. I wanted to go check if he practiced nearby, but my stomach fizzled at the thought. We hadn't talked last night. I'd darted straight for our cabin after the sing-along.

I would never know if I stayed put. I stepped out of the practice room and the tone of a familiar female voice drifted down the hall. A giggle escaped from the room and the doorknob twisted. I needed to get out of there.

I turned back the other way, but the door opened faster. "Geri!" Her shrill tone pained my ears. I didn't understand how her singing voice could be so much more beautiful.

I bit my bottom lip and pivoted. "Hi, Chloe."

Chloe turned back to the open door. "Thanks for the help, Ethan. See you later."

She glanced back at me, and I saw nothing but scheming in those blue eyes. So much for being non-enemies.

"See you at practice in a few." She walked out the door.

"Oh, hey, Geri." Ethan peeked out of the practice room. "You went through with the idea?"

Ethan stepped into the hallway. "I asked you the other day. You said you were fine with me helping Chloe out."

I nodded. "Right." I was *not* fine with the arrangement.

Ethan came closer. "I'm sorry for walking off yesterday. I guess I got jealous, but I understand." He put his hands around my waist. "Who better to help you compose than a composition major? It's like me helping out Chloe."

I pushed him back. "Me working with Tyler is *not* like you helping Chloe. She's your ex."

Ethan put his hands in his pockets. "Yeah, *ex* being the key." He furrowed his eyebrows. "Geri, we've been over this."

I shook my head and closed my eyes, hoping the motion would bring me somewhere else. "I can't deal with the drama right now."

He came closer to put his arms around me again, but his arms felt stifling instead of comforting. I pushed back. "I need to practice."

"You want help?"

"I need to do this by myself." I managed half a smile. "But thanks." I reversed down the hallway.

"Geri," Ethan called.

I turned around.

"Are you OK?"

"Yeah. Fine." *Yeah, not fine.*

When I got back to the practice room, I went through the piece a few more times. The melody sounded good, but the tone needed to be more dynamic. I played with the piece, adding a *crescendo* and *mezzo-forte* there, and a *decrescendo* and *mezzo-piano* there.

After several run-throughs, I needed a stretch break. Laughter trailed from outside the window, and I stood to peek through the glass. Hannah, Niki, and Julia walked down the path. Colorful pieces of pottery rested in their hands. Teambuilding without me. Thanks, guys. Wait, since when did I care about teambuilding? And I did tell Hannah I needed to practice. Then why did my throat feel tight?

The clock on my phone read 10:30. Time for one more run-through. I wiggled my fingers over the keys but hesitated. I never did get input on the piece. Maybe Tyler came in, and he could listen. Ethan acted all buddy-buddy with Chloe. I could have Tyler listen to me.

I walked to the office and poked my head in the door. The cords of his earbuds lied strewn on his desk next to the keyboard and a bowl of mints. I forgot he had the day off. My stomach gurgled. Maybe skipping breakfast hadn't been such a good idea. Tyler wouldn't mind if I took one piece of candy.

I stepped into the office and grabbed a mint. Next to the bowl sat a pile of papers. The first one read "*Why I Should Win the Scholarship* by Chloe Evans." The entry counted as 20% of her score. Without the essay, she couldn't win. Shouldn't they have locked those things up?

I held the paper in my hand. Applause and cheering echoed in my head from Chloe's performance last night. Geri, you can't. The essay deadline ended at noon, in a couple of hours. Without the submission, she'd be disqualified. *I need this more than you, Chloe Evans.*

I folded the papers and tucked the essay under my shirt. I sped down the hallway into my practice room and stuffed the secret in my bag along with the old copies of my composition.

I threw in a pencil along with the papers and left. Disqualifying Chloe meant I had my chance at winning back. A girl's gotta do what a girl's gotta do. She'd have done the same to me, right?

My gut twisted as I walked down the path to our cabin. Did my stomach flop because I'd missed breakfast or was the distress from something else?

CHAPTER 24

My heart beat as fast as my speed-walking legs. I turned the corner with the guilt of stealing Chloe's essay burning deep in my soul. I needed to escape the papers before they scorched me like the summer sun.

"Geri!" Hannah met me on the path.

I froze, clenching the bag tighter, afraid Hannah could see through the fabric.

"You're just in time for practice." Hannah motioned in the direction of the dance studio.

"I'll put my stuff in the cabin first." I pointed in the other direction.

Hannah scrunched her eyebrows. "Don't you need the music for practice?"

"I ... I ..."

Hannah grabbed my elbow. "The girls are already there, went straight from the pottery studio. I looked for you to join, but figured you were busy composing up a storm."

And practicing my kleptomaniac skills.

Hannah pulled me down the trail and away from the safety of the cabin. I tried to create an excuse to flee, but my brain remained frozen.

The studio's air conditioning seemed extra chilly when we entered. I didn't need more frigid conditions. My heart had already turned into a block of ice, unfeeling and willing to do anything to win.

When we entered the room, Hannah grabbed my tote. "Put your bag by the piano. I promise no one will steal it." She put the evidence on the floor and gave me a teasing smile.

I swallowed and sat on the keyboard's unsteady bench. Why had she used the word steal? Did she know? My eyes darted to the tote bag. A dust bunny hovered near the opening. Thank goodness fuzz couldn't talk.

"Attention, girls." Hannah clapped her hands together. "This is it. We've got everyone here to put the whole piece together with the actual music."

Julia and Niki joined Hannah in the center of the studio. Chloe leaned against the mirrored walls, typing on her phone.

"Chloe, you ready?" Hannah rested a hand on her shoulder.

She put her cell down and stood, tugging at her mini skirt before plodding to center stage.

Hannah motioned to me. "Geri, come join us."

I walked over and stood next to the girls, turning my eyes to the ground.

"Let's clarify the choreography," Hannah began. "The piece opens with Julia's ballet number. Eight bars, right ladies?"

Hannah had such kind eyes. She would never steal someone's essay. Could she tell I had from the look in mine?

"Then eight bars of Niki's piece." Hannah looked between Niki and me. Neither of us argued, and she continued. "Next we have a few battle bars until the dances collide. Finally, we end with Chloe singing to accompany the new piece while Julia and Niki dance at the same time. Is that right?"

We all nodded.

"Remember we have to be flexible since this is our first run-through with the music." Hannah clapped twice. "Places everyone."

Julia took center stage, Niki stood off to the side, and Chloe and I made our way to the side with the piano. I sat at the keyboard, and she went back to the bench, submersing herself once again in her phone. She didn't look my way, but her silence didn't surprise me. It's not like we had reached best friend status. Or maybe she knew her stolen essay lay a few feet from where we sat. Scratch that. If Chloe knew I'd stolen her essay, her hands would be on something else besides her phone—like my puppy throat.

The worn pages of the piece Tyler and I composed stuck out against Chloe's crisp essay in my bag. I took out the music, careful not to let any of her papers slip out. I put the score on the keyboard stand and placed my fingers on the keys.

"Ready Julia?" I glanced at her.

She nodded her bun-topped head, and I began *Rondo Alla Turca*. We'd been through the dance dozens of times over the past few days, but I played the music instead of the speakers. *Pas de boureé. Chassé. Saut de chat.* Julia leaped through the air. *Entrechat. Entrechat. Entrechat.* She crossed her toes in midair while jumping three times and then began her turn sequence. Her body whipped around in circles before ending with another gigantic leap off stage left.

Niki stood on the side ready to enter. I began the part of the music Tyler and I slaved over, turning hip-hop into something the piano could handle. While I played, Niki danced. Her right hand pumped in the air as she jumped and tucked her feet underneath her body. She spun around and kicked out her toes. Her legs crossed in and out while her arms did the same. The moves didn't line up perfectly, but with practice we could get there. Niki ran a few beats before leaping across the floor switching her legs in midair. She landed with a rare smile.

"What do you think, Niki?" I rested my hands on the keys.

She walked over to me. "Good music, girl." She patted me on the back. "We'll practice getting the piece show-ready."

I let out the breath I had been holding. "Oh, good. I'm glad you like it."

Chloe sighed from the bench.

Niki turned toward her. "Something wrong, Chloe?"

She scratched her throat with her left hand and kept typing with the right. "My throat is getting tight sitting here waiting."

"You want us to skip ahead to your part, Princess?"

She put down her phone. "Sure. And let's run through once *without* the distraction of the dancers."

Niki looked at me. "Seriously?"

I shrugged. I had stolen Chloe's future. The least I could do was let her sing.

Niki shook her head and walked back toward Hannah and Julia. "Dance break. Chloe needs to sing. She's getting bored."

"Finally." Chloe smoothed her skirt. "Hannah, where are the lyrics again?"

Hannah dug through her bag.

A piece of paper fell to the ground as I turned the pages of the score. I glanced at the sheet from Chloe's essay. My head filled with the sound of my beating heart.

Now I'd done it.

I looked around to see if anyone had noticed. Hannah flipped through her notebook while Chloe watched. Julia marked her combination, and Niki lied on the floor with her eyes closed. Napping maybe?

An oscillating fan blew the paper a few inches forward. I snatched the essay before putting the secret behind the other papers on the keyboard. Good thing the solo only took up one sheet. No page turning needed.

Chloe stood in the center of the room, her posture tall. Drops of sweat slid down my forehead. I brushed them away and shook my head to focus.

"I'm ready!" Chloe announced to the entire studio. She pushed the sleeves of her sweater to her elbows. I took a deep breath and began playing. Thoughts of betrayal clouded the melodic unity. I stared at the sheet music, but the picture of Chloe's essay burned through the page.

I must have been distracted because I hit the wrong note. Chloe recognized the mistake right away and marched over to the keyboard, fixing her hands on her hips. The scar peeked out from the right sleeve of her sweater.

"What's with that note?"

I averted my eyes before she noticed I had been staring at the papers. "Which one?"

She crossed her arms and the scar disappeared into her annoyance. "*There were highs*," she sang. "*Highs*." What do you have there?

I looked back at the music. "I have a G."

"That's what I'm singing, isn't it? *Highs*."

I played the note. The tone matched. "Yes."

Chloe scrunched her eyes. " Then let's try the song again, the right way."

"Right."

Chloe walked back to the center. "From the top!"

We started from the beginning of her solo. I tried to concentrate better.

"*There were highs!*" Chloe sang and lifted her right arm to the sky. "*And there were lows.*" Her left arm pointed down in the direction of my bag.

The motion rang true. I considered stealing beyond low, but how I could I win without disqualifying her? I didn't see any other way.

CHAPTER 25

Sweat dripped down my face. I had only been in the heat for a few minutes, but I'd also committed a small crime. Or maybe two if you count breaking and entering. Is eating someone's mints also a crime? Then I had three offenses.

I'd convinced the other girls to go to lunch without me, even though I hadn't eaten all day and I had to ward off Hannah's concerned motherly looks. My phone buzzed in my bag, and I jumped. My tote and its contents dropped to the floor of our cabin, including Chloe's essay.

I picked up the interruption and looked at the caller. Dad. No thanks. I had enough emotional torture. I pressed the side of the phone to make the flashing stop and dropped the black screen in my bag.

Chloe's scholarship submission and fate still lay on the floor. I picked up the essay, unsure what to do with the evidence. Should I drop the papers in the lake? Visions of soggy shreds floating back to shore entered my mind. Throw the pile in the fire? Soon I saw charred pieces flying all over camp. Put the indictment in my suitcase? What if Chloe went to borrow my clothes? Fat chance. Chloe would never want to borrow my clothes in a million years. They didn't shine and covered my rear end. Two things she would contest against.

A knock came at the door while Chloe's essay seared into my hands. I scanned the room for a quick hiding spot, my heart pounding in my chest. Nothing seemed feasible. The knock sounded again.

I hid the papers behind my back and opened the door with the other arm.

"Hey." Ethan smiled. "I heard you could use an escort to lunch."

"Lunch ... yes. Ummm ... give me a minute to change. I'm super sweaty." I closed the door before he could respond.

"Close one," I said aloud and picked up the paper. With the prospect of Chloe needing clothes from my suitcase slim, I decided the safest spot for the essay rested there.

I was headed for the door when I remembered the promise to change out of sweaty clothes. I slipped on a fresh T-shirt and applied a few swipes of deodorant, however, the clean shirt didn't cover up the feeling of my dirty little secret. I zipped the suitcase for good measure and walked out of the cabin.

Ethan's broad shoulders faced me. His biceps stretched tight against his light blue shirt. I needed a distraction. I wrapped my arms around his waist and pressed my face against his side. He put his arm over my shoulder and kissed the top of my head. "Ready?"

I looked up and smiled at him. "Yup."

He grabbed my hand, and we walked toward the cafeteria. A slight breeze rattled the tall pine trees, and a bird sang somewhere in the distance. I breathed in the moment when everything seemed right in the world.

Ethan squeezed my hand. I stood living my music dream with my dream guy by my side and—then he dropped the "C" bomb.

"You don't mind if I help Chloe out once in a while, right?"

"What?"

He looked at me. "Chloe. Sometimes she needs accompaniment to practice."

Chloe. Stealing her essay in my bag. My boy—Ethan, wanting to help her. Everything stunk in the world.

"Umm ... sure ... I guess." What else could I say? I'd already stolen her future. Giving her accompaniment seemed like the least I could do when her performance without the essay wouldn't matter anyway. A thought surfaced.

"Ethan?"

"Yeah."

"Remember during the volleyball game when Chloe wouldn't play, and you told her you would tell everyone what you'd found in her bag?"

"Yes."

"What *was* in her bag?"

Ethan chuckled. "A teddy bear."

I thought of my cherished teddy bear hidden underneath the sheets. "That's not the worst thing ever."

"No, but if you haven't noticed, Chloe likes to put up this tough girl front. I knew the threat held enough weight to get her to play."

I looked at Ethan. "You really would have told everyone?" I kicked a rock sitting on the path. Why did I care?

"I knew I wouldn't have to, but no, I wouldn't have told. That gift is special to her. Her first foster family gave her the bear. From what she's told me, she felt like she belonged there, but she had to leave."

"How come?"

Ethan shrugged. "I'm not sure. We dated for a while ..." His eyes met mine. I tried to encourage him to keep going. The look must have worked because he looked back to the path and continued. "Once in a while, I could get something out of her, but she doesn't talk about her past much."

The topic of Chloe already held the conversation. "And the scar?"

Ethan took a deep breath. "I'm not sure. I know she's had the mark since childhood. I have a feeling the burn caused her to be separated from her biological family. They took her out of the situation, but she'll have that scar forever."

I was the Worst. Person. Ever. Chloe didn't deserve to be disqualified.

I looked up at Ethan. "What time is it?"

He took his phone out of his pocket. "12:37."

I gulped. The essay deadline had passed.

"Are you all right, Geri? You look pale."

"I'm fine," I muttered. My empty stomach didn't feel hungry anymore.

"Thanks for coming here with me." I dipped my paintbrush in the cup of water.

Abby brushed another stroke of blue onto her ceramic bowl. "Of course. Every girl's Friday night dream." Abby looked around the empty room. "*Claro*."

"I needed to calm my nerves. Art and music relax me." I added more purple to my plate. I needed to practice, but now when I thought of the competition, I thought of how I'd sabotaged Chloe.

"Are you still nervous about Ethan? He really does like you, you know."

I put down the brush. "No, I'm not upset about Ethan." I needed to tell someone what I had done. Regret bubbled in my stomach. I couldn't take the guilt anymore.

Abby added a yellow rim to her bowl. "Then what's the painting about?"

"There's something I have to show you."

"Go on ..." She tilted her head to the side.

I grabbed her hand. "Right now."

"What about my pottery?"

"Let your bowl dry until morning. No one else is coming in here tonight."

"I guess you're right."

I put both of our brushes in the water cup. "C'mon."

I pulled Abby out the door and down the path to our cabins. "Geri, you're scaring me."

"That makes two of us."

"Very comforting."

We finally reached Cabin Twelve. I hoped nobody stood inside because I had no Plan B. We walked through the door, and I flicked on the light. All clear.

"You're showing me your cabin?" Abby looked around. "Great. The room looks very similar to mine. Must have been the same architect." She smiled.

I unzipped my suitcase. "This is no time for jokes, Abby. This is serious." The essay burned my palms.

"All right, tell me then because I don't know what has you—"

I shoved the essay in her hands. She read the top line aloud. "Why I deserve the scholarship by Chloe Evans." She scrunched her eyebrows and looked at me. "Are you proofreading this for Chloe? Is that what you're trying to tell me? You two are best friends now?"

"The deadline passed at noon."

"So, you're not a very good friend because you didn't return the paper in time?"

"Think worse." The room spun, and I sat down on Hannah's bunk.

"I don't get what's going on." Abby handed the essay back to me.

I stood and held up the papers. “I stole this. I took her entry out of the office in the music studio. I disqualified her.” My face burned, and I fought back tears.

Abby’s eyes bulged. “¡Ay! You did what?”

I sat back down and put my hand over my face. “I know. I’m the worst person ever. I don’t know what came over me. I have to get the essay back. I have to fix this.”

Abby walked over and sat next to me. She put a hand on my shoulder. “*We* have to get the essay back. *We* have to fix this.”

I wiped away a tear. “You’re going to help me?”

She put her arm around my shoulder and hugged me. “We’re in this camp thing together, remember? Even when you’re *loca*.”

I sat up. “Thanks, Abby. I know the act screams crazy. I really messed up.”

She smiled. “Yeah, but you know you messed up. Admitting your mistake counts for something.”

I gasped and stared at her. “What if we can’t return her entry?”

“There’s no room for doubt. Instead, we need a plan.”

CHAPTER 26

I woke to the sound of the bugle horn. My head popped upright and hit the ceiling. I rubbed my forehead. Bunk beds. Yet another reason I didn't like camp.

"Did you get hurt up there?" Hannah tapped the side of my bunk.

"Nope, I'm good." I rubbed the top of my head.

"Up-and-at-'em," Julia sang as she jumped off her bed.

A pillow flew out from the bunk below, threatening to knock the ballet slippers off her pajamas.

Chloe sat up and stretched to the ceiling. The sleeves of her pajamas slid down her arm revealing part of the scar. She put her hands down and straightened the shirt to cover her wrists.

My head fell back on my pillow, and I remembered I had failed at life. I'm not sure how I forgot my crime in the thirty seconds I'd been awake. I'd tossed and turned most of the night, afraid we wouldn't be able to return the essay, and I'd further ruined Chloe's life. Even with the plan.

I sat up again, careful not to knock my head again. How much time did I have before the master plan went into action? I titled my phone up. 8:01. Twenty-nine minutes until I met Abby.

The wooden beams of the ladder met my feet as I climbed down. Go time. I slid my suitcase against the wooden floor, careful not to let anything else fall out while I grabbed my clothes.

"Everyone ready for breakfast?" Hannah stepped out of the bathroom pulling her hair into a ponytail.

"I'm ready." I turned around to see Julia in a pair of jean shorts and a white T-shirt.

Niki moved under the sheet over her head. She lived after all. "Tell me when we're leaving, and then I'll get up."

Chloe typed on her phone ignoring us. Her foot rested on the opposite knee as she jiggled her bright pink toes back and forth.

I pulled on my T-shirt and then heard a tap on the window.

"Company before breakfast?" Niki mumbled from under her blanket.

Julia stuck out her long neck. "Looks like Geri's boyfriend to me."

Then Chloe decided to stop ignoring our cabin.

Chloe rummaged through her suitcase and pulled out a pink sundress. I felt like I competed in a race. For what? To see who could kill Ethan with morning breath first? I ran to the bathroom, gurgled toothpaste and water, and rushed out the door.

On the way out, I bumped into Chloe and her monstrous make up bag fell on the floor.

"Watch where you're going, Geraldine." Great, now I physically hurt her too.

"Sorry," I muttered.

I grabbed my phone out of my pocket. 8:14. I had sixteen minutes until I needed to meet Abby.

Hannah rattled Niki's foot still under her sheet. "We're leaving now, Niki."

"You guys go ahead. I'll catch up with you later." I kinda fibbed. I would meet up with them later, but not at breakfast. Add another charge to my rap sheet.

Niki sat up. "Don't keep the guy waiting."

"As long as your promise to eat breakfast. I didn't see you in the cafeteria at all yesterday." Hannah's brow furrowed.

"I'll eat. Promise." I didn't lie completely. I'd eat at some point, depending on how long the plan took. I smiled at Hannah and slipped out the front door.

Ethan leaned against the wooden post, his damp caramel hair shining in the morning sunlight. He turned when he heard the door open and flashed a gorgeous smile. "Hey, Beautiful."

I put my arms around him, and I soaked in the sandalwood smell of his freshly washed hair. Seeing him brought a mixture of emotions. I delighted in having an incredible guy care enough to see me first thing in the morning, but his presence also made me feel guilty. I pulled at my T-shirt. What would he do if he knew I had stolen Chloe's essay? Would he ever talk to me again?

"Need company at breakfast?"

"I—"

Before I could answer, the door opened again and Julia, Niki, and Hannah appeared.

"Hey, Ethan." Hannah waved. "Joining us for breakfast?"

"In a minute." Right, now I lied.

"Barbie's on her way." Niki rolled her eyes as she walked past us.

"At least she cares about her appearance." Julia went down the steps.

"What are you implying?"

"I'm not implying anything."

Niki and Julia continued down the path, practicing their argumentation for the talent show.

Ethan grabbed my hand, and his sparkling blue eyes met mine. "Ready to go?"

Before I could answer, the door opened and Chloe, or should I say Elle Wood's twin, appeared. The V-neck on her pink dress plunged beneath her black cardigan.

"Oh—hey, guys." She put her shoulders back, further accentuating her cleavage. Real classy.

Ethan squeezed my hand. "Chloe, you look ..."

I looked up at him. Choose wisely, sir.

"Ready for the day," Ethan finished.

Safe choice.

"Thanks." She batted her mascara-coated eyelashes and stepped down the stairs in matching pink wedges. Her hips swung from side to side as she walked toward the cafeteria.

Did I really need to return the essay? I shook my head. Yes, yes I did.

Ethan tugged at my hand. "Let's go. Unless someone else is coming out of there."

Only my guilty conscience.

"Ethan, thanks for coming to get me for breakfast, but I'm going to grab something from the Snack Shack on the way to practice. The talent show is in a couple of days, and I need the music to be perfect."

"Practice can wait until after breakfast." He tucked a loose strand of hair behind my ear. Man, he was convincing. I wanted to drift away in those blue eyes, drift away from camp and the talent show and the Chloe scholarship sabotage.

I pulled away. "I'm sorry. I have to do this."

"But Hannah is expecting to see you there."

"I promised her I'd eat, and I will."

Ethan sighed. "At least let me walk you to the Snack Shack then."

I took my phone out of my pocket. 8:20. Ten minutes until I needed to meet Abby.

"Give me a minute." I'd already made a billion excuses. Besides, I wanted to walk with him. "Let me grab my music." And the essay.

I went back into the cabin and took the essay out of hiding. I stuffed the papers in my tote bag between sheet music and put the bag over my shoulder. Stay closed bag. Stay closed.

I walked back out the door, and Ethan and I headed toward the Snack Shack. The morning sky reflected a bright blue with puffy white clouds, the exact opposite of my mood.

"Geri, watch out for the—"

Unforgiving dirt slammed against my back. The tote bag slipped from my shoulder, and incriminating confetti littered the walkway. No, no, no!

Ethan bent down to help.

I reached for the stack. "I'll pick up the mess. I'm the clumsy one who—"

Ethan cut me off. "What is this?" He held a piece of Chloe's crumpled hope.

Deep breath in. Deep breath out.

"I'm returning her entry. Promise." I reached for my dirty secret, but Ethan pulled back.

"Why do you have Chloe's essay?"

"I ..." I didn't want to lie to Ethan, but the truth weighed down my tongue.

"Why do you have Chloe's essay?" His voice raised.

I held my breath. Once he found out, our—whatever we had—would end.

"Did you take this, Geri?" His eyes blazed like blue flames.

I couldn't put the truth off any longer. I nodded.

Ethan held the paper in the air. "Are you out of your mind?"

"I don't know. I need to win to get to Juilliard."

"At Chloe's cost?"

"I'm returning the essay. I have a plan."

Ethan turned around. "I don't believe this."

I put my hand on his back. "Ethan, I—"

He faced me, holding the evidence of my downfall. "Your plan better work."

I took the papers and gulped.

"You know where the Snack Shack is. Find the rest of the way yourself."

A tear slid down my cheek. I'd ruined everything. I'd sabotaged Chloe and lost Ethan, all in a matter of twenty-four hours.

I watched him walk away, holding the essay to my chest. The time on my phone read 8:28. In two minutes Abby and I would start the mission to return Chloe's entry, and then I would start the mission to get Ethan back.

Reasons I Don't Like Camp—

13. Bunk beds

14. Small crimes

CHAPTER 27

"You're late." I followed Abby's voice to the music studio's stairs. Abby sat crouched down beside the worn wooden steps wearing a black T-shirt and shorts.

I pointed to her outfit. "Aren't you going to be hot in your costume?"

She pulled at my T-shirt, and I plopped to the ground. Then I also appeared sketchy by the stairs.

I rubbed the back of my sticky neck. "Isn't this suspicious?"

Abby put my hand over my mouth and hissed into my ear. "*Silencio*. Somebody will hear you."

"Sorry." I matched her voice level.

Abby slid sunglasses from the top of her head to her nose. "Phase One. We need to see if the you-know-whats are still in Tyler's office."

"You mean the essays?"

"Shhh!"

I looked around the area of the music studio. "Abby, there's no one out here."

"Not yet."

Who did she expect? Spy Kids to join our posse?

"Here. Put these on." She handed me a pair of skinny black sunglasses.

"Do I really need to wear these?"

"No, but disguises make the mission more fun."

I shook my head and slipped on the glasses.

Abby's head moved from side to side. "Where's Tyler's office?"

Several windows lined the wall acting as our concealment. Although anyone that turned the corner from the front door of the studio would see us.

I followed the building with my finger. To get to Tyler's office, I walked down the hall and turned left. We couldn't see the other side of the building from our hiding spot.

I lifted my tote bag back on my shoulder. "His office must be around the back."

Abby wobbled along the side of the building like an oversize crab. "*¡Vámanos!* Let's go."

I followed, trying not to look ridiculous, but the effort didn't matter. The whole ordeal oozed ridiculous.

"Wouldn't finding the office be easier if we walked upright like normal people? This is killing my calves." I used my fingers to balance myself on the grass.

Abby continued to speak in a low voice. "We're supposed to be at breakfast—well I am. You're supposed to be doing whatever excuse you gave. We can't let anyone see us."

I rolled my eyes. Soon we reached a large bush at the edge of the building. Abby disappeared inside the bristly hideout. Seriously? The branches scraped against my arm as I followed her.

Abby turned to me through a sea of leaves. "I'm going to see if anyone's around the other side." The shrub rustled as she peeked through the greenery. "The coast is clear."

I followed, teetering out of the bush. More scraping. If the piano thing failed, I could always turn into Sebastian. I would play a mean clam shell drum set.

"Is this the crime scene?" Abby pointed to the window above our heads.

I rolled my eyes at her dramatic choice of words. "I'll check."

Abby patted my back. "Go, Geri."

I looked around before standing up on my now sore legs. My hands gripped the windowsill as I rose on my toes to see inside. Blond ponytail. Pink dress.

I ducked down next to Abby.

"Did you see his office?"

"Worse." I grabbed Abby's arm.

"His office without the essays?"

I shook my head.

"What then?"

"Chloe," I mouthed.

"What's glowing?"

I tried mouthing the words again.

"Slowly?" Abby scrunched her eyebrows.

"Chloe," I scream whispered.

Abby's eyes bugged out of her head. "Didn't she go to breakfast?"

I shrugged and pointed forward, hoping she'd get the hint to keep going. She did, and we waddled to the next window.

"I'll check this time." Abby moved her head side to side. She stood up on her tiptoes, straining her calf muscles. As she peeked in the window, her long braid touched the middle of her back. She looked down and gave me a thumbs up.

"What about the essays?" I patted my tote bag.

She crouched back down. "They're still there. I see a pile of papers on his desk and no sign of Tyler. There's no reason they wouldn't be there." Abby scanned the area. "Time for Phase Two."

Abby stood, and I copied her.

"Now, look nonchalant." She pulled her braid in front of her shirt.

I surveyed Abby in her black clothes and sunglasses. "Like you?"

She smiled. "Exactly."

I pointed to the right. "Let's go the opposite direction of Chloe's window."

"Good call."

Abby and I walked around the other side of the building. I opened the front door, and we entered. No instrumental sounds flooded the entryway, which seemed strange and added to the secret mission ambiance.

Abby took a step and the wooden floor squeaked.

I grabbed her hand. "I don't want Chloe to hear us and come out."

"She's not supposed to be here either. Maybe she won't come out of the room."

"Maybe." My stomach flopped.

We tiptoed down the hallway. When you're doing something you're not supposed to, time drags. You would have thought we had to pass a hundred rooms instead of five.

We turned down the hall on the left. I heard Chloe's unfortunate angelic voice as we passed by her practice room. At least her solo covered our squeaky steps.

The next door held Tyler's office. Abby pointed to the closed entrance.

I nodded.

She put her hand on the handle, but the knob didn't budge.

"Are you sure?" I tried the door myself. No luck. My breath got quicker and shorter. The room spun.

Abby put her hands on my shoulders. "Geri, *Cálmate*. I have an older sister who lives in the bathroom." She pulled a bobby pin out of her hair. "I got this." Abby stuck the end of the minuscule tool in the door handle.

I glanced down the hall. Quietness replaced the tune behind Chloe's door. She had stopped singing.

"Hurry!" I leaned against the wall to steady myself.

Abby leveled her eye with the handle. "The lock's trickier than the one at home."

I heard the ping of the doorknob, and at the same time, Chloe's room opened.

"Ta-da!" Abby lifted the bobby pin in the air.

I kicked her.

"Hey, Chloe," I put on the biggest fake smile I could muster.

Abby turned her back to Tyler's office.

"What are you guys doing here?" She put her hands on her hips.

"W-w-we should be asking you the same question." I rubbed the back of my sweaty neck.

"I'm practicing."

Without Ethan? What an idea!

"Yeah, us too." I pulled the tote over my shoulder.

Chloe moved her head toward Abby. "You're practicing?"

"Moral support." Abby smiled.

Chloe scrunched her eyebrows. "Right."

She took a step near us, and I clenched my tote bag.

"Since we're both here let's practice our piece together. The song needs a lot of work."

"I need to play the music by myself first." I pointed to Abby. "With moral support."

"Haven't you been working on this all week?"

"The notes aren't perfect yet. There are chords I want to fix to fit your voice better." The flattery burned my throat, but the possibility of secrets surfacing trumped the sick feeling.

Chloe's blue eyes narrowed. "I guess, but you don't have much time. The talent show is in a few days."

"I'll get the harmony all sorted out this morning before practice. Promise." If she only knew I needed to sort out so much more.

Chloe pursed her lips. "Fine." She turned and walked back down the hall. Her wedges escalated the squeaks in the floor until I heard the front door close.

I slid my back down the wall and sat, clutching the tote bag. "Way too close."

"You're telling me." Abby turned the doorknob of Tyler's studio. "*Voilá*!"

"Are the essays still on his desk?" I followed Abby into the office.

"Yup." Abby picked up the same pile I'd seen yesterday.

I grabbed Chloe's essay out of my bag. Smudges of dirt dotted the creased top sheet. I grabbed a tissue from Tyler's desk and tried to wipe away the evidence. The gesture helped, but the essay didn't look the same as it had before.

I held up my best effort. "Good enough?"

She looked over my pathetic attempt. "It has to be. Plus, they're more interested in the content than the way the paper looks."

"True." I laid the essay on top of the pile. Chloe's entry looked misplaced and disheveled among the clean copies. I lifted the stack halfway and stuck submission between the others, hoping the weight would help flatten the paper.

I let out a deep breath and turned to Abby. "There. Mission accomplished."

She grabbed my arm. "I told you we would."

I turned toward the hallway. "Let's go."

We walked out of the office but before I closed the door, I looked back at the pile of essays content Chloe's rested with the others. Now I'd have to win the real way, by being the best. When had I ever been scared of a musical challenge before?

I shut the door. Never.

CHAPTER 28

Mission One—Return Chloe's Essay. Check.

Mission Two—Get Ethan back. Still in progress.

As I walked back from the music studio, my chest felt tight. What if Tyler had already done a checklist of the essays last night and Chloe's would still be disqualified? What if Chloe found out what I'd done? What if Ethan didn't forgive me?

Speckles of morning sunshine colored the dirt path. Abby had rushed off to catch the end of breakfast, but I didn't feel like eating. I still felt embarrassed about what I had done. I couldn't imagine facing everyone. My stomach rumbled. Practice would be starting soon, but I needed to eat something.

The Snack Shack stood close by. I figured the building would be empty at breakfast time. Of course, I had to see everyone at practice, but I'd worry about facing the group later. I held my stomach. Food first.

The smell of buttery popcorn hit me when I opened the Snack Shack's door. I walked to the counter. Popcorn for breakfast sounded pretty good. Maybe my day was looking up already.

"Hey, Geri, didn't see you in the cafeteria." Hannah appeared next to me. Her cheery expression contrasted against my crumminess.

I turned toward her. She wore a smile, but her eyes drooped. I couldn't lie to Hannah. I'd already done enough wrong to last a hundred movement concerto.

"Yeah, I didn't go. I decided to come here instead." I faced the counter, hoping my truthful response would appease her.

Hannah put a hand on my arm and led me to a table. "Geri, is everything good with you? You've seemed ... off ... the last couple days."

I sat down and took a deep breath. Part of me wanted to open the story and spill the truth of its pages, but fear sealed the book closed.

"The days here have been hard." My eyes felt warm as the truth of the confession set in. Camp had been an emotional roller coaster.

Hannah rubbed my arm. "Totally understandable. New place. New faces. New guy." Her emerald eyes glistened.

I wiped away a tear rolling down my cheek. I didn't know if I had a guy anymore.

Hannah squeezed my hands. "But you've accomplished a ton, creating a blueprint for our number, composing music. Geri, you're rocking camp!"

If she knew all the other things I'd done ...

I shifted in the plastic chair. "Thanks, Hannah, but I haven't done everything right."

"None of us have, Geri. We just do our best."

"And what if our best messes up?"

Hannah smiled. "We do what we can to make the situation right. Then we keep going, knowing we'll mess up again because we're human."

I sighed. "That's strangely comforting."

"Yeah, and remember, we don't have to walk through life alone."

I thought of Abby in her black getup and sunglasses. "True."

Hannah pointed to the counter. “Want to get something to eat?”

My stomach gurgled. “Definitely.”

After another practice session, Julia and Niki’s parts improved. Chloe and I could use more time to work on the ending, but first things first.

My knuckles burned from all the useless knocking. No one answered. I sat on the porch of Ethan’s cabin, squinting at the sun moving behind the pine trees.

I put my chin on my knees. If I were Ethan where would I be? A bird tweeted above. I snapped my head up. When I’m down, I go to music. Maybe Ethan did the same.

My legs peeled off the wooden stoop as I stood. The back of my shirt stuck to my skin, but I didn’t care. I needed to clear things up with Ethan. My heart thudded as I walked to the music studio. I wandered the halls, peeked into each open room, and strained my ears to the possible plunks of a guitar. No Ethan.

I leaned against the front door and tapped my fingers on my forehead. Where could he be? Music still seemed to be important in the equation. Guitars are mobile. He could play anywhere. The lake?

I headed in the opposite direction. When the path ended, I shuffled through the grass to the water. Ethan’s muscular frame sat a few feet from the edge, a silent guitar in his lap. He sat as still as a photograph, his chin resting on top of the instrument’s frame.

I took a deep breath. Time to apologize. The squeak of my flip-flops eradicated any chance of making a quiet entry. He turned when I got closer, and then looked back at the water.

His silence showed he didn't want to talk to me. I stepped backward. Any ounce of confidence faded. I couldn't face him. As I retreated through the grass, I tripped on my sandals and fell. Why so clumsy? Always.

Ethan turned after my rear end hit the unforgiving ground. "Geri! Are you hurt?"

Possibly—of embarrassment mainly. I winced.

He swung his guitar over his back and rushed over. He reached out his hand, and I stood. Maybe he didn't completely hate me. Hope bubbled in the pit of my stomach.

Apologetic word vomit exploded from my mouth. "Ethan, I'm so sorry. I should have never taken Chloe's essay. The decision qualifies as cruel and unusual punishment. I returned her entry. If I had a redo, I wouldn't take the paper. Promise. I don't blame you if you hate me and never want to speak to me again, but please, please do."

He crossed his arms. "You're right. Taking Chloe's essay is messed up."

"Yeah, I know." I grabbed my flip-flop. "Look, I'll get going. Leave you to your ... whatever you were doing here."

Ethan's eyes softened. "Thinking about you."

I slipped my sandal through the wrong toes. "What?"

He grabbed my hands. My little toes burned with the plastic strap through them, but I didn't care.

"Yeah, what you did was ..."

"Stupid, mean, horri—"

Ethan cut me off. "I've done my share of stupid, mean, and horrible things too."

"Name one."

His eyes turned upward. "Last summer, Aiden and I knew the girls next door to us were afraid of frogs so we made frog noises outside their window."

I shook my head. "A prank isn't the same."

"You're right, but what I'm trying to say is everyone does dumb stuff."

"Then you forgive me?"

He wrapped his strong arms around me. "Of course, Geri."

My eyes felt warm. I pulled back to face him. "Best news all day."

"You and Chloe are going to be best friends now, right?" He smiled with a goofy grin.

I pushed him. "Um, no. Let's not get carried away."

"Speaking of carried away ..." Ethan had a gleam in his eye I did not appreciate.

He placed his guitar on the grass. Not a good sign. Within seconds, my feet flew off the ground, and Ethan carried me toward the water.

I gripped his neck. "Now Ethan. Let's not do anything irrational here. I'm not wearing a swimsuit or anything."

The water got closer.

"Does it look like I care?" Ethan laughed.

"What if I can't swim?"

"Can you?

"Are you willing to find out?"

We reached the dock.

"I'll take my chances."

I held tighter to his neck. "ETHAN!"

My window to reason with him ended. All my sweaty stickiness kerplopped into the lake. My head emerged from the water. "You actually threw me—"

Before I could finish, Ethan jumped in.

He brushed his wet hair backward. "You're welcome."

His wet T-shirt clung to his body, and my anger melted. After all, he had just forgiven me for trying to sabotage his ex-girlfriend.

I swam closer to him. "There's a way to make it up to me?"

His eyes twinkled. "How?"

"You know."

He smiled, moved a few inches closer, and kissed me and all my imperfection. Somebody knew my flaws and liked me anyway. A swim in the lake didn't get much better than complete rejuvenation.

Reasons I Like Camp–

8. Impromptu swimming in the lake

CHAPTER 29

Chloe stood with her shoulders back, and her head held high. Her voice reverberated through the studio. Perfect pitch. Exactly what the judges would want.

Chloe remained in the scholarship running. The list of contenders hung on a bulletin board in the music studio. When I saw her name, I felt relieved, but also nervous. She should compete, but her voice threatened my chances.

"You found me and wouldn't let me fall." As Chloe sang a wrong note, Julia and Niki ran into each other. They fell to the ground, and Chloe crossed her arms. "I told you we need more practice, Geraldine."

Julia stood and smoothed her ballet skirt. "I thought we decided I'd move to center stage. You were supposed to go in the back."

Niki jumped off the ground. "Why? So you're the star?"

Hannah clapped her hands. "Girls, girls. We're putting too much pressure on ourselves. You've come a long way." She motioned for us to come center stage, and we gathered around.

She put one hand on Chloe's shoulder and one on my own. "We'll master the choreography in the couple practice sessions we have left. Let's take a fifteen-minute break. I'll stay with Niki and Julia to work on the choreography while Geri and Chloe work on the solo."

Chloe's eyes darted toward me. "I told Geraldine yesterday we needed to practice."

What she didn't know was I'd spent the time requalifying her for the scholarship. Bet she wouldn't be sour if she knew that. But then she would know I stole the essay in the first place.

"Fine with me." Niki turned to Julia. "We need to find a way to showcase the both of us."

Julia put a bobby pin back in her bun. "My talent will always shine, Nicole."

Niki rolled her eyes.

"Great." Hannah smiled. "Way to keep up the characters, Niki and Julia. Let's take fifteen, and then resume our individual practicing. We'll meet back here in an hour, and try the piece as a group again."

Chloe turned toward me, and her ponytail flipped in the same direction. "Let's go to the music studio. I don't need a break, do you? We need to utilize our practice time."

Less time with Chloe seemed more enticing, but she had a point. We needed to hammer out her solo to be ready for the talent show and to win the scholarship. Either one of us.

"Fine." I avoided her gaze, still worried she would be able to tell what I did if our eyes met. I turned my attention to the keyboard, grabbing the sheet music and my phone.

We walked to the music studio in silence. What is there to say to your guy's dream-stealing ex-girlfriend who you tried to sabotage?

After several minutes of quiet, Chloe spoke. "We should look at the key when we get there." She tapped her throat. "The melody isn't fitting my voice."

Remember, Geri. You need *her* to look good for *you* to look good.

"Right, the key. We'll look at the notes first."

We arrived at the building and checked with Tyler for an available room.

"Room Three's open," he pointed down the hall.

"Sound good, Chloe?"

She studied me. Guilt makes you do nicer-than-normal things.

Tyler pointed at her and cocked his head. "Wait, Chloe. Chloe Evans?"

Chloe leaned back on her hip. "Yes."

Tyler picked up the pile of essays and rummaged through them. My heart hammered in my chest.

He displayed a dirty crinkled essay. "Is this yours?"

My throat felt dry, and I coughed in my fist. Tyler peered at me, scrunching his eyebrows.

Chloe stepped forward to examine the paper. "That's mine, but I didn't turn my entry in like this."

"Maybe I dropped a pile on the floor. I'm clumsy. The thing is ..." Tyler turned to the last page. "Did you mean to stop here?"

Chloe snatched the essay from him. Her eyes grew wide. "No! This isn't the ending. A piece is missing." Chloe flipped through the papers. "Where's the last page?" She looked at Tyler.

The room spun and my stomach churched. I leaned on the wall for support and clutched the cover-up. The last page could be in my tote.

"Geri, are you feeling all right?" Tyler peered at me.

"I need some air." I walked into the hall and emptied the bag's contents. Sheet music. Sheet music. Sheet music. My heart stopped.

The last page of Chloe's essay.

A tear appeared in the top left corner where the page had broken away from the rest of the stapled papers.

Chloe's shrill voice pierced my ears. "How can I win with an incomplete essay?"

"Do you have another copy?" Tyler held up the wrinkled pages.

"No, I don't have another copy! I turned in the whole thing. Someone did something with my entry!"

If I confessed, I might lose the scholarship, but how could I live with myself if I knew I'd blow Chloe's chances? The air left my lungs. I needed to do something.

I took a deep breath and turned the corner, still holding the last page of the essay. I held the missing piece with a shaky hand. "Here's the last page."

Tyler's eyes narrowed as he looked at the paper. "What? How do you ..."

Chloe came toward me like a high-speed train. "Let's state the obvious." She stopped before crushing me, her red face inches from mine. "She took my essay!"

Tyler scrunched his eyebrows. "I don't get it."

I looked at my shoes. "I returned the paper, but I didn't know I missed a page."

"I don't understand," Tyler ran a hand through his hair.

"I do. You want the scholarship. You were trying to better your chances." Chloe held the papers close to my face.

I rubbed the back of my neck. "I ..."

Chloe turned toward Tyler. "There has to be a rule against this." She pointed her long pink fingernail at me. "She should be disqualified."

Tyler scratched his head. "I don't know. This hasn't ever happened before." He took the paper from me. "We'll add the last page back to your essay though."

Chloe clenched her entry. "And that's going to make the situation all better? I'm going to make sure action is taken. I'll go talk to Maury myself."

"You don't have to ..." Before Tyler could stop her, she dashed out the door. My stomach sank as I heard her stomp her wedges toward a conversation and my scholarship-less fate.

Tyler stepped into the hall. "Chloe!"

Calling after her landed flat. The door slammed on the studio and on my chances of going to Juilliard.

Tyler came back into the room. "What happened?"

I slid down the wall, clutching the tote bag. My eyes felt hot, and I tried to hold back tears. I'm a horrible person. An unforgivable person. A horrible unforgivable disqualified person who could kiss Juilliard goodbye.

Chloe had gone through a lot, more than I would ever know, and I'd tried to take more from her. My phone buzzed. I needed a distraction from the horrible unforgiving moment.

Dad again. I silenced the ring and stared at the cell in my bag.

"Geri?" Tyler's voice brought me back.

"I wanted to win so bad." A tear trickled down my cheek.

Tyler sat in front of me. "You're talented. You didn't need to steal to win."

"I know. I'm horrible. The act is unforgivable."

"You're not a horrible person, Geri. Good people mess up too."

My phone chimed with a voice mail. I looked at the glowing screen in my bag. Good people do mess up. My dad used to be a good person. Before he messed up big time. I wanted a redo. Did he want one too?

"I need to go," I stood up and slung my bag over my shoulder.

"What? Where?"

"There's something I need to do." Before I walked out the door, I turned around. "Tyler?"

"Yeah?"

"I'm really sorry."

His face softened. "I know you are, Geri."

My heart raced in my chest as I turned the corner. When I walked through the front door, I opened my recent calls. I took a deep breath before pressing Dad's name.

Jenna Brooke Carlson

Reasons I Don't Like Camp–

15. Losing my chance at Juilliard.

CHAPTER 30

The lake glistened in the afternoon sun. A few campers canoed in the distance, their laughter floating to the shore. I swished my legs in the cool water while I sat on the edge. Abby lounged with her feet stretched straight out, flexing her toes back and forth.

She tilted her head back. "Big day tomorrow."

"Yup." I dripped cool water on my arms.

The talent show premiered tomorrow. Camp activity had stopped as everyone prepared for the performances. Eat. Practice. Sweat. Swat bugs. Worry about being disqualified. The routine summed up my day.

"You ready?"

"To be disqualified?" I kicked my foot into the water. "No."

Abby put her hand on my shoulder. "You don't know you won't be able to compete."

"As soon as Chloe finds Maury when he gets back to camp, she'll tell him. She hasn't spoken one word to me all day. She's probably saving them to prosecute me in court."

"Isn't her not talking to you a good thing?"

I turned to look at Abby. She smiled and raised her eyebrows.

"Usually, yes." I shrugged. "But not when she's conspiring against me."

"You technically conspired against her first."

"Hey." I pushed her. "You're not helping."

"It's true. If something does happen, I know who will be more than happy to console you." She nudged me.

I splashed water on her. "You're unbelievable."

"And right. I told you Ethan wasn't like your dad."

My dad. I hadn't told Abby I called him back.

"Speaking of ..."

"Ethan has a secret available twin."

"No ... speaking of my dad ..."

She clutched my arms and shook me. "*¡Santo Cielo!* You're speaking of your father. Have you also adopted a pet spider?"

I rolled my eyes. "No. I called him."

"What? Why?"

"He's been calling since I got to camp. I've never answered, and I don't know. I just ... called him back."

"And?"

"And ... nothing really. I told him about camp."

"Geri, this is huge!"

I missed him. We had father-daughter ice cream nights before ... everything.

"Is he coming to the show tomorrow?"

I shrugged. "I don't know."

"Do you want him to?"

"Still don't know." But I did. And I did care for some odd reason. Guess your dad is still your dad even after he messes up.

Footsteps pounded behind me before stopping near the lake.

"Last teambuilding exercise." Hannah peered over my head. "You ready?"

Niki, Julia, and Chloe trailed behind her. I would have rather gotten a pet spider than do more teambuilding with someone who threatened to vanquish my dreams.

I looked up at her. "Ummm ..."

She looped her arm through mine and pulled me to my feet. "Team activities aren't a choice. Let's go." Hannah made commands sound sweet.

"I'd better get going too. *Buena suerte*. Good luck." Abby patted my back before leaving. I needed luck. And maybe a miracle too.

"*Now* will you tell us what we're doing?" Chloe placed her hands on her hips.

Hannah nodded toward the nearby lake house. "Kayaking!"

Chloe and I groaned.

"And you two are going to be partners," Hannah pointed between us.

My eyes widened.

"Not a good idea." Chloe stared at me, her lightsaber eyes ready to cut me in two.

"Nonsense." Hannah took my arm again and shuffled me next to Darth Wedge-Parader. "Teambuilding is just what you girls need. Work together to learn to *work together*." She smiled.

"You expect me to kayak in this?" Chloe held out her white mini skirt.

Hannah waved a hand at her. "You sit. No big deal."

"What if I fall in?"

Hannah smiled. "Don't." I liked sassy Hannah.

She turned to Julia and Niki. "And you two will be partners. We're working with our partner in the performance." She punched her hand in the air. "One more boost of bonding before our big day."

"I'm game." Niki stretched her arms across her chest. "I spend summers at my aunt's lake house."

"I haven't been in a kayak before, but how hard is steering a small plastic boat?" Julia tilted her chin toward the air.

Niki pursed her lips. “Mmm-hmm.”

“Your goal is to paddle one time around the lake with your partner.” Hannah made a circle with her finger.

We also needed to survive one time around the lake without killing our partner. How about we take the whole kayaking thing out altogether and go with ‘Don’t get killed by your partner’? Much more feasible.

“Mission accepted. Let’s do this.” Julia walked toward the boathouse. Niki followed.

Chloe folded her black sweater arms.

“Go ahead, girls.” Hannah flicked her wrist. “The kayak isn’t going to appear by magic.”

Chloe rolled her eyes and marched her wedges across the grass. I sighed and went with her. We’d bond quickly. And if meshing didn’t work, I’d call Flagstaff PD. Did they do lake rescues?

We arrived at the boathouse and approached the counter. Julia adjusted the short life vest on her tall frame. Niki clipped the buckles across her chest before they both walked out the door. Chloe snatched a jacket from the hooks and smashed the orange-covered foam over her head.

I copied her, but less like I wanted to hurt somebody. Chloe headed out the door, and I tagged along afraid to upset the monster any further.

The kayaks sat clustered in a green blob by the dock. A tall counselor stood assigning to campers. Chloe and I walked down to the pier.

“Here you go.” The counselor slid a kayak in front of us.

I looked at the dirty plastic bottom. “We’re supposed to get in that thing?”

The counselor laughed and placed two paddles on the side of the pier. “You’ll survive. Promise.”

I eyed Chloe’s shoes. “You’re going to need to lose the wedges.”

She huffed in response.

The counselor opened her mouth, but then closed it again. "I'll hold the boat while you get in."

Chloe paused before taking the counselor's offer. The frame wobbled as she placed her wedged foot inside. The counselor winced as Chloe steadied herself in the front seat while trying to tug her miniskirt over her rear end.

"Nice work. Have fun." The counselor walked off to help another set of campers.

Wait. What about me?

Chloe grabbed a paddle from the pier then straightened her dishtowel-sized skirt.

I cleared my throat, and she didn't turn.

I wore flat shoes, but I still couldn't magically jump inside.

"Chloe." I stomped on the dock.

She focused her gaze on the water. "Why should I help you? You did the opposite to me."

I took a deep breath. "Look, I'm sorry." Did I just apologize to my archenemy? The situation couldn't get any worse. Oh yeah, she planned to rat me out me and ruin my dreams. The day could definitely get worse.

I paced back and forth on the pier. "I did a stupid, horrid thing. I shouldn't have touched the pile, let alone taken your essay. If I could turn back time, I would."

Chloe didn't move.

I stopped pacing. The apology approach didn't work. I thought for a second.

"The quicker I get in, the quicker the trip will be over." I sighed.

A loose hair blew in the breeze, and Chloe tucked the strand behind her ear. She turned around and grabbed the pier. Her hot pink nails stood out against the weathered wood. "Get in then."

I kicked off my flip-flops and put a bare foot in the kayak. Gross, but the gesture lessened my chance of slippage. The canoe rocked, and Chloe gripped the pier tighter. "Hurry before I break a nail."

I sat on the tiny seat behind Chloe and put my other leg inside. Whew. I made it in one piece.

"Grab your paddle, and let's get this over with." Chloe unbuckled her lifejacket.

"You're supposed to keep the jacket on."

"Orange is not my color." She slammed the life vest on the kayak floor.

Had she just hinted I might go to prison for stealing? I decided to keep my mouth shut and grabbed the paddle, ready to get the awkward ride over with.

How about I dump Chloe and head for Juilliard instead?

Um, yeah. I'd definitely be wearing orange then. Would Ethan come visit me?

CHAPTER 31

Chloe and I attempted to kayak without speaking. Our paddles clashed mid-air when we picked the same side. For being a singer, she had no sense of paddle rhythm.

I placed the end of the stick on my knee. "Maybe we should count the strokes like music."

"Or you could keep up."

I let her try by herself, and we moved at a snail's pace. Hey, worked for me. I leaned back ready to put my feet up when Chloe turned around.

"What are you doing?" Her perfectly shaped eyebrows scrunched together.

"Letting you have your way."

Chloe hit the water with her paddle. "Fine."

She faced forward again. "Let's count." So, she *had listened* to me.

The paddle felt heavy in my hand. "Let's paddle on 3,4 on the right and 7,8 on the left."

I took her silence as an agreement.

"1, 2, 3, 4," I began. We fumbled with the counts at first, but after a few bars, we moved in the same direction.

"5, 6, 7, 8," I repeated.

"We can count in our heads now, Geraldine."

"Whatever you say." My tone dripped like the camp pancake syrup.

The kayak glided through the lake, and the shoreline came into view. Campers milled around on the beach, and a group of guys played volleyball in the shallow water. Maybe Ethan roamed up there.

I couldn't identify Ethan, but I noticed someone else right away. Maury. He stood in the distance, but I could spot his round belly anywhere.

My paddle swished to a steady rhythm, but my mind raced. As soon as Chloe saw Maury and placed her pedicured feet on land, my plans would collapse. My dreams vanquished.

"Oh, good. Look who's back." The corners of Chloe's mouth turned upright.

My stomach dropped. The edge of the lake stood a few yards away. "We need to turn, Chloe."

"We need to go to the shore." Her paddling *accerlerando*ed, and our counts suffered.

The kayak wobbled. I held the sides to keep my balance. "Easy."

"I want to talk to Maury now."

I took a deep breath. "Fine." I couldn't put off my fate any longer. "But let's go back to the dock. Getting off will be harder up there."

"Turn around then." She directed me as if I supposedly knew how.

"1, 2, 3, 4."

"Stop counting. Just paddle."

We stroked our paddles to an uneven rhythm. They clashed against each other, and the kayak tilted.

"Geraldine!" Chloe screamed.

"I'm trying." The boat's edge dipped closer to the lake.

Chloe jerked her paddle back and forth, rocking the kayak. Water splashed my bare feet.

"You need to calm down or we're going to—"

Too late. The kayak tipped over, and Chloe screamed like she'd found out only one Dalmatian remained in the whole world.

I tumbled over the side after her, the cool water submerging my body. My life jacket helped me reach the surface.

I wiped my eyes and caught a glimpse of Chloe. She flapped her hands, spattering water in my face.

"Will you quit splashing?"

"I don't know how to swim."

My heart rate accelerated.

Chloe bobbed up and down, her eyes wide and panicked.

I lunged myself out of the water and yelled for help, hoping someone could hear me. Chloe's lifejacket floated in the water. I grabbed the life-saving device and swam to her.

I pushed the ounce of hope between us. "Grab on."

Chloe reached for the vest but missed.

"Take the jacket, Chloe."

She tried again, unable to take hold of the orange promise. Her head titled back, an inch from the surface.

"Geri! We're coming!" Ethan ran to the shore.

A lifeguard jumped into the lake. He swam behind Chloe with a rescue tube. He leaned Chloe on the tool and rushed back to the shore. Ethan helped pull her out of the water and onto dry land. She lay silent a few moments before she coughed and gasped for air.

I'd never been so happy to see an enemy undefeated.

Chloe slept in the white linen sheets on the nurse's office bed. Her usual pristine hair reached across the pillow in frizzy waves, the dirty blonde tresses turning lighter as they dried.

I bobbed my foot up and down, willing her to open those fiery blue eyes. Even though Chloe remained my enemy, she still was a person. I wanted her to be all right. I wrapped the worn striped towel tighter around me.

"Are you sure you don't want to go back to your cabin and change?" Ethan rubbed my shoulder.

Nurse Sandy felt Chloe's wrist and jotted notes on a clipboard.

"After she wakes up. I need to know she'll be all right." I squeezed Ethan's hand.

The nurse walked over to us. "She'll be fine. Just needs her rest."

"Are you sure?"

She smiled. "She had quite the accident for sure. But you got her help in time."

Abby burst through the door. "I came as soon as I heard." She took my free hand. "Are you OK, Geri? How's Chloe?"

"They'll both be fine." Nurse Sandy pressed the clipboard against her chest. "But it's a good thing Geri yelled for help when she did. Drowning only takes seconds."

"I heard a scream on the beach and grabbed a lifeguard." Ethan's thumb grazed the top of my hand.

Abby let out a heavy sigh. "*Gracias a Dios.*"

Chloe stirred, and her eyes fluttered open. "What happened?"

Nurse Sandy walked to the cot, putting her hand on Chloe's forehead. "You had a fall in the lake."

She sat up, revealing her blush pink hospital gown and matching scar. "I need to practice."

Nurse Sandy shook her head. "You're not going anywhere. I want to keep an eye on you tonight."

Chloe cleared her throat. "But the competition is tomorrow."

"You should be fine by then. This is only a precaution."

Maury walked in the door. "How's the patient?"

Chloe pulled the blanket over her scar.

"She'll be fine after she rests." The nurse helped Chloe fix her sheets.

Maury stood next to the cot. "You gave us quite a scare, young, lady." He looked at me. "Both of you."

Chloe seemed to spot me for the first time. She peered at me before her eyes grew wide. "Maury, there's something I want to tell you."

My stomach dropped.

Ethan stood. "Good thing Geri screams as well as she plays. She saved both of you."

Chloe's eyes darted back and forth between me and Maury.

"Yes, Miss Evans?" Maury shifted his weight.

Chloe's gaze settled on me. "Umm ..." Her icy blue eyes melted. She looked back to Maury. "Never mind."

My eyes felt warm. She decided not to rat me out? We hadn't crossed the finish line in the kayak race, but Chloe's silence told me we'd turned a corner.

Reasons I Like Camp–

9. A new chance at the scholarship

CHAPTER 32

My sandal-laden feet plodded across the camp stage, heavy from the immense pressure of the moment. The sheet music in my hand trembled as I placed the page on the piano's music stand.

Deep breath. Bach. Mozart. Beethoven.

I straightened my light pink skirt across my lap, its floral pattern twisting and turning to the stage's floor like my stomach. Beethoven. Bach. Mozart.

Campers lined the first few rows. Parents packed the rest of the logs. My mom sat near stage right. I attempted to smile at her. Moms always knew where to sit to see their kids.

A long folding table holding three judges stood in front of the crowd. Two men wore white collared shirts. One fixed his bowtie and the other adjusted a pair of glasses from the tip of his nose. The woman fingered a white pearl necklace lying on top of a bright blue dress. Those three individuals held my fate. I gulped.

Julia poised in the front of the stage, her long arms postured in a perfect circle around her black leotard and peach ballet skirt. She nodded at me before dipping her head. I stretched my fingers over the piano's white keys and took a deep breath. All the hours of practicing had led to the critical moment.

Mozart's *Alla Rondo Turca* began, and Julia dragged her toe against the stage floor. I didn't need the sheet music anymore, but the notes on the paper provided comfort. Julia's dedication paid off. She moved strong and precisely. I didn't have ballet experience, but to me the sequence revealed perfection.

The music transitioned to Niki's part, and she entered from stage right. I played the "E Flat" chord in eighth notes while Niki's feet marched to the beat. I added the higher notes with my right hand, and Niki began a series of jumps I'd watched her practice over the last week.

I turned my attention to the judges. Hannah had promised she would mention I had composed, with help, the last two-thirds of the piece on the entry form. The man with the bowtie nodded while taking notes. The woman stared straight ahead looking unfazed, and the man in the glasses held their rim before turning his attention toward me. I darted my eyes back to the music, even though I didn't need to see the melody. I played the last few bars of *Ronda Alla Turca* and turned the page.

The "battle" had begun. Julia spun like a top on fire, her peach skirt swirling around her. She landed and turned her gaze to her opponent. Niki's arms punched the air, her quick feet matching the *allegro* speed of the piano's rhythm before kicking both legs in the air and landing in a warrior position. The performance came to life as both girls brought their off-stage attitudes to the piece. The audience probably thought they acted out their parts, but I knew better.

The intensity of Julia and Niki's performance grew while their showcased time intervals shortened.

Julia. Julia. Julia.

Niki. Niki. Niki.

Julia. Julia.

Niki. Niki.

Julia.

Niki.

Julia.

Niki.

My hands melded the ballet and hip-hop pieces together in the masterpiece Tyler and I had created. Soon Julia and Niki danced in unison. As they moved backward, Chloe walked on stage in her iconic white skirt and a flamingo pink top. Her matching wedges pounded against the wooden floor until she stopped in the center.

Chloe placed her arms at her sides, the ruffles of her black sweater cascading to her hips. Her chin jutted out as she held her head high and stared straight ahead. She looked like an angel. Too bad she sounded like one too.

I played the beginning notes from Hannah's song and Chloe sang. Her melodic voice sounded smooth, yet strong. The music reached the modulation, and Chloe stepped forward, using her hand movements to emphasize the words. Applause and shouts rang out from the audience.

My eyes moved again to the judges. This time all three of their gazes transfixed upon Chloe. They seemed captivated by her exquisite voice. I considered messing up on purpose to break their hypnotized gazes, but a screwed-up performance wouldn't have worked out well for me either.

I turned my attention back to the keys. I decided to put all I had in the last few lines of the music. My body moved with the chords, coming closer to the piano on the accentuated notes. I needed the scholarship. I needed them to see me behind Chloe's magical spell.

The last few notes of the composition rang from the piano. In the end, I suspended my hands above the keys. Cheers rang from the audience, and the crowd jumped to their feet. I wished they clapped for me, but no one watched the girl on the piano. They stared at the girl with an angelic voice.

I turned my attention to my mom who stood beaming. Unlike the rest of the crowd, her attention fixated on me. Moms are always proud of their kids.

My eyes continued to wander over the audience. Most of them clapped while smiling and cheering for Chloe, except for my dad. My *dad*?

He stood by the other side of the stage, but near the front. He also clapped and smiled ... but looked at *me*.

My cheeks felt warm, and I turned back to the stage. My cabinmates all stood in the center, and Niki motioned for me to join them. I walked to the middle but kept my eyes down. I was glad my dad came, but I hadn't seen him in weeks. I didn't know what to do with myself.

My chest expanded as I took a deep breath and walked to the center of the stage. Julia stood in between Niki and Chloe with her arms draped around them. I slipped mine around Chloe's shoulder along with the black sweater. My heart pounded as I embraced my biggest rival and potential downfall.

We all took a bow while the judges smiled. I let go of Chloe as we walked off the stage. I'm not sure which made me more uneasy, facing my dad at the end of the performance or finding out the results of the competition.

The applause faded and we walked down the stage's steps. Hannah greeted us first.

"Amazing job, girls!" She gave us all hugs.

"Thanks." I squeezed her back before returning to the front row.

"*Magnifico*," Abby whispered to me.

I didn't say anything but instead turned my attention back toward the stage. The piece had been great, due to Chloe's majestic voice. My stomach flipped.

Abby grabbed my arm. "You know the piece screamed amazing, don't you?"

I looked straight ahead. "I know Chloe sounded remarkable."

Abby patted my leg. "True, but you performed an extraordinary piece too."

The next cabin began their number. I pretended to watch their tap dance performance, but my thoughts swirled. Chloe. Scholarship. Dad. Juilliard. Dad.

Abby squinted at me. "There's something else," she whispered.

Thank you, Best Friend Syndrome, for not letting me hide my thoughts.

I tilted my head to the right in the direction of my dad. She turned her eyebrows downward and looked in the same direction. I watched her eyes move back and forth before they stopped and grew wide.

"He came," she mouthed.

I nodded. Abby squeezed my hand and smiled. I turned my eyes toward the stage to watch the rest of Cabin Thirteen's performance, but I couldn't concentrate. I felt the same during the next two performances. My body sat on the bench at camp, but my mind drifted elsewhere. What would happen when I saw my dad again?

The instrument-clad girls from Cabin Fifteen ended their number, took a bow, and walked off stage. They received applause, but nothing like the resounding ovation after Chloe's solo. The cheering died down when Maury walked on stage.

"Campers, parents, loved ones, thank you for attending our talent show today. Didn't they do a great job?" Applause and enthusiastic shouts rang from the audience. "Our performance is over, but a few of our campers have applied for a music scholarship to the school of their choice. We will allow the judges to deliberate, and then, they will announce their decision tomorrow. Thank you again for coming and drive home safely."

"The performance is over, but I'm still nervous." I stared ahead.

"Are you talking about seeing your dad or the scholarship?" Abby placed a hand on my shoulder.

I turned toward her. "Both. I don't know what to do. Who do I go to first, my mom or my dad? Will the second one get their feelings hurt?"

Abby shrugged. "Wait for one to find you?"

I shuffled my sandals in the dirt. "What if the first person is my dad?"

"Say hi?"

I pushed my palm in my forehead. "This is impossible."

Abby put her hand on my shoulder. "*Estâ bien*. You'll be fine, Geri. Promise. Want me to wait with you?"

I looked at her. "No, go to your mom. This is something I need to do on my own."

"All right, are you sure you're OK?"

"Fine." But I wasn't.

Abby stood and walked away. I sat alone as all the other campers found their parents. My hands felt clammy on the wooden bench. I can do this I told myself. My stomach flopped. I cannot do this, I retold myself.

"Geri."

Dad.

He had on his usual denim pants and plaid shirt, and a dark shadow grew around his mouth and chin.

"Hi, Dad." I stood, and my heart thumped to a continuous rhythm in my chest.

He smiled and squeezed my hands together. "You did good, kid. You wrote the music?"

I rolled back and forth on my sandals. "Part of the melody."

"That's what the program says." He held out a white piece of folded paper.

I took the pamphlet and scrolled through the order of performances. Cabin Twelve. *Alla Rondo Turca* by Wolfgang Amadeus Mozart. Original music by Geraldine Bruchi with assistance from Tyler Voss. They sold Tyler short but seeing my name as a composer felt amazing.

"My daughter, the composer." My dad straightened his back and put his hands in his pockets.

The moment of silence seemed to last for an eternity. Finally, I opened my mouth, "Dad, I ..." I looked down at his white gym shoes and back to his tall frame.

In the blink of an eighth note, I wrapped my arms around my dad's waist, his flannel soft against my face. "Thanks for coming." I took in the scent of burning logs on his shirt. Dad always liked campfires and roasting marshmallows. Maybe I got my love of s'mores from him.

He put his strong hands around me and hugged me back. "Wouldn't miss your show for the world, kid."

My stomach flipped. "Wanna go get ice cream?"

"Definitely."

I opened my eyes to see Mom smiling in the distance. As I held my dad, I still doubted securing the scholarship, but I knew something for sure. I'd already won at this.

Reasons I Like Camp–

10. *Good performances*
11. *Dad's surprise*
12. *Father-daughter ice cream*

CHAPTER 33

I sat at my usual piano in the music studio. My fingers had to be lively to keep up with Chopin's composition, but my brain felt groggy from the lack of sleep. Plus, I hadn't had any time to practice the sonata since I'd arrived at camp. The notes felt rusty.

I ended the piece and laid my head on the keys. My stomach lurched. I couldn't take much more of the anticipation. I'd spent all night replaying our performance in my head, the mesmerizing look on people's faces as Chloe sang. I needed to know the results already.

A knock sounded at the door. I lifted my head in time to not look pathetic as Ethan walked in.

"Hey, beautiful." He smiled.

"How did you know I would be here?"

He put his arms around me. "Great musicians think alike. You knew where to find me when I felt stressed." His embrace eased the discomfort, but the uneasy thoughts still lingered.

I took his hands and turned around to face him. "I'm nervous, Ethan. What if I don't win the scholarship?"

He squeezed my hands. "You'll find another way."

"I don't know another way."

"You would find one, and hey, you haven't lost yet. The big reveal is at noon."

I looked down at my feet. “Yeah, and they are telling the winner in person first which means if no one comes by, I didn’t win.”

Ethan tilted my chin up with his finger. His bright blue eyes sparkled. “Hey, no matter what happens, you did amazing, and you’ll get to Juilliard.” I would believe anything while peering into those eyes.

He kissed me and for a second all thoughts of the scholarship disappeared. I opened my eyes when he pulled away. I returned to the practice room and the piano, camp, and the competition.

“Now, let’s get breakfast.”

I stood. “No way. I’m going to be in my cabin all morning. I cannot miss those judges.”

“See, you are still positive you’ll win.”

“You’re forgetting another candidate is in my cabin.”

“Right.” He paused. “Want me to bring you something from the cafeteria?”

“Thanks, but I can’t eat.”

“I understand.” He squeezed my hands. “I guess I’ll see you at the big reveal then.”

I put my sheet music back in my bag. “Yeah, the big reveal.” Had Mozart and Chopin gone through this misery?

I paced around the cabin like Bach in jail. 1, 2, 3, 4, 5, 6, 7, 8. Turn. 1, 2, 3, 4, 5, 6, 7, 8. Turn.

“Geri, will you stop pacing? You’re making me crazy.” Julia peeked over the top of her bunk.

“Let her work off her nerves.” Niki scrolled through her phone.

The wall stood in front of me, and I turned again.

Hannah grabbed my arm. "Do you want to talk or something, Geri?"

I began my paces away from her. "Nope, I'm good."

Meanwhile, Chloe sat in her bunk flipping through a gossip magazine, but when I say flipping, I mean more like trying to set the world record for the most pages turned in a minute. The sound of the paper accompanied my walking.

A knock at the door made me jump. I froze. Did the sound signal the end of my misery or the beginning of a deeper scholarship-less pain?

"Geri, you've been walking for a half hour. Open the door." Julia pointed in the direction of the tapping.

Hannah stood from her bed. "I'll get it, Geri." My feet stood glued to the wooden floor.

The open door revealed the two male judges. I felt sick. Hannah greeted them and invited the fate deciders in.

"Good morning ladies," the one in the glasses said. "May we speak with Chloe Evans outside please?"

My stomach dropped to the floor. I'd lost. To Chloe.

Chloe threw her magazine on the bed and jumped to the ground. Her shoes clunked on the wooden boards, and I twitched. "Of course, gentleman."

The judges walked back out to the porch, and Chloe followed. My eyes felt hot, and the room spun. I needed to get out of there.

"Geri, are you OK?" Hannah stepped toward me.

"Fine." I dipped past her and out the door. Keeping my head down, I shot past Chloe and the judges.

"Congratulations, Miss Evans," I heard one of them say.

"Thank you." Chloe's voice oozed with unrecognizable sweetness.

"Miss Bruchi, are you leaving?" I heard from behind me.

I wiped a tear from my eye and turned around. "I need to take a walk." I tried my best to smile.

"May we have a word first?"

A word now? When a surging waterfall pooled behind my eyes? The tears threatened to gush out and knock the judges to their feet, sending them and their horrific scholarship news far from camp.

I pointed to myself. "With me?"

"Yes," the judge with the bowtie grinned.

"Ummm ... sure." I rubbed the back of my neck and went back toward the porch, trying my best to hold in the tears about to explode.

The judge with the glasses began. "We normally only tell the winner the results. Want to be secretive you know? But this is a special case." He paused at looked at Chloe. "Miss Evans here has won our scholarship." Chloe beamed, her ponytail seeming extra high as she stood tall.

I forced a nod. Now if he didn't mind, I wanted to get on with my meltdown.

He patted the other judge on the back, "But Mr. Erwin has noted your tremendous composing talent."

I appreciated the compliment, but the words couldn't make up for what I'd lost. Plus, the talent show program hadn't given Tyler justice. He'd done more than assisted me with the composition. Honesty boiled out.

"I had help with the music."

The judge adjusted his glasses. "Yes, we spoke with Mr. Voss. He assured us you do have the talent we saw on the stage."

Mr. Erwin continued. "Yes, Miss Bruchi. I would like to extend the invitation to come to our composition camp next summer. We have all the best teachers and of course, instruments."

They wanted me to go to summer camp?

Again?!

"The camp is in New York, a pristine location."

New York? Juilliard. My ears perked up.

"Many of our attendees go on to the best music schools. All expenses paid. We have your contact information from your entry. May we call you in the coming weeks with more details?"

"Yes, of course." I wiped my tears. My eyes hadn't caught up with the good news.

The judges shot me confused expressions as if they wondered why I still wanted to cry. I'd lost the competition, but I had a new opportunity in front of me. Maybe composition camp could help.

"Great." He smiled. "We'll leave you, ladies, then. We'll announce your winnings at the camp's send-off, Miss Evans."

We watched the judges walk off, and I stood next to Chloe unsure of what to do with myself. She'd won. I hadn't.

"Congrats, Chloe."

"Thanks." She rubbed her black sweater arms.

"And thanks for not ratting me out for the whole ... you know, essay thing. I wouldn't have this chance at composition camp if I'd been disqualified."

Chloe crossed her arms. "Since I'm the best from the talent show, I guess you can be the best at composing. Hunching over writing music all day would be horrendous for my posture."

You could have good posture while you composed, but I accepted the semi-nice comment.

"You're going then?"

"Where?"

"To the composition camp?"

I leaned against the wooden porch. "I don't know. The invitation sounds like a good opportunity, but I'm not a fan of camp."

Chloe displayed her white shorts and pristine shoes. “I’m not a fan of camp, but you have to do what’s necessary to make your dreams come true.” Her bright blue eyes darted to the sky before looking back at me. “Why did you want the scholarship in the first place?”

“To go to Juilliard.”

Chloe pursed her glossy lips. “That camp can help you get there. You should go.”

Her curly ponytail swished behind her as she turned and went inside. I still hadn’t been offered any money, and I still didn’t how I would get to Juilliard, but I knew one thing.

Better stock up on bug spray. I’d be headed to camp again next summer.

Reasons I like Camp–
13. Composition camp surprises

CHAPTER 34

I rolled my suitcase one last time on camp grass. Until I went to camp next summer. The wheels bounced on a rough patch of dirt, and my pillow fell from the top.

"I'll get that." Ethan appeared next to me. He picked up the pillow and wrapped the ends around my face. "Like the first time we met." He smiled.

I grabbed the pillow and shoved him. "I'm shocked you still spoke to me."

"What are you talking about? That's what made me fall for you." Ethan turned up the corner of his mouth and revealed his dimple.

"Ha. Ha." I returned the pillow to the top of my suitcase. My forehead felt clammy from my too-hot-for-camp jeans. Hannah had said I could keep her shorts, but room didn't exist in my camp baggage for Hannah's shorts and the memories of Ethan's defined muscles.

Ethan pulled his duffle bag over his broad shoulder, his biceps visible in his cutoff T-shirt. I pushed my sunglasses to the top of my head and gazed into his crystal blue eyes. I wouldn't be able to see him every day after we left.

He scrunched his eyebrows. "What's wrong?"

"We're leaving." My eyes felt warm.

Ethan dropped his bag on the ground and laced his fingers in mine. "We're only an hour away from each other. I'll come up next weekend. Promise."

"Sure." I trusted him now. "Since you're promising and everything."

Ethan wrapped a wisp of my hair around his finger before tucking the strand behind my ear. "I keep my promises." He tilted my chin and kissed me. The butterflies in my stomach did not want me to leave camp. My clammy forehead, on the other hand, readied for the exit.

"*¡Apúrate!* Hurry up your goodbyes now." I spotted Abby over Ethan's shoulder. "Time to go."

Ethan pulled me in close, and I tried to trap the smell of sandalwood in his hair. The rush of campers leaving muted for a few seconds while I held Ethan tight. Everything seemed right at that moment.

A car horn broke my trance, and I pulled away. "She's right."

"When am I not right?" Abby set down her bag. She pointed between the two of us. "This. Right here. Called that."

I raised the handle on my suitcase. "All right, Abby."

Ethan put up his hand. "Wait, wait, wait. I didn't hear any of this before."

I grabbed Abby's hand. "And we're not going to start now. C'mon, Abby. You said we had to go."

"We have time for one short stor—"

I pulled her in the direction of the parking lot before she could finish. After a few steps, I turned back around. Ethan still stood in all his athletic-built glory. I couldn't leave him just yet. My pillow and suitcase dropped to the ground as I ran back to him.

"So, you do want to tell me the story."

"No." I wrapped my arms around him tighter than Chloe wears her mini dresses. "I needed to say goodbye again." I felt safe in his embrace. Could I stay at camp with Ethan forever? Sweat trickled down my forehead. Well, maybe change the month to September, a light cool breeze, maybe we wouldn't have to be at camp per se ...

"We'll see each other soon, remember?" Ethan's voice brought me back to About-to-Fry-July.

"I do." I wiped a tear from my cheek.

Ethan smiled. "Call you later, then."

"Yeah." I looked to my feet. I needed to get out of there before the waterworks started. We hadn't known each other long enough for Ethan to see *that* side of me. "Bye." I squeezed his hands before letting go and then walked back toward Abby.

"Geri, you owe me a lot for this summer." Abby rose on her toes and stretched her calves. "And you didn't want to come."

"What do you want me to say, Abby? You're right about everything in the entire universe?"

"I don't know about the entire universe, but I'll take credit for camp, and Ethan and your willingness to go back to camp even if going means more bugs—"

"Girls!" I looked over Abby's shoulder to see my mom waving from the parking lot.

"But you can thank me later. *Vámanos.*" Abby set off for the car before I could respond.

I tilted the suitcase forward and began walking. I looked over my shoulder to where Ethan had been. He fist-bumped one of his buddies. How did I get so lucky? He was sweet and sensitive and strong and—

Wham! And striking. I hit the ground.

A long manicured hand stuck out to me. "Geraldine, you should watch where you're going."

I looked at Chloe's outreached arm before taking the offer and letting her help me up.

"Thanks. I'll try."

I brushed off my jeans and smoothed my T-shirt.

"And Geraldine?"

"Yeah?"

"Go to camp next summer. You can't waste opportunities. Plus, with you not around, winning another competition is a breeze." Chloe whipped her ponytail back around and leaned into her right hip, picking up her conversation with her posse.

A bead of sweat trailed down my forehead as I bent down to pick up my pillow. Was that her way of being nice? I shrugged. I'd take the compliment.

I made my way to the car. My world had changed since I'd seen the blue sedan last week.

"Did you have a good time, honey?" Mom took my suitcase and pillow from me. Her short bob strained to form a ponytail at the back of her head.

"Yeah, I did."

"I'm glad, but I'll be happy to have you back at home." She hugged me before going to the front of the car.

I climbed into the back seat next to Abby and shut the door.

"Did you get lost?" She pulled out an earbud.

"No, I ran into Chloe. She told me to go next summer."

"Go where?" Mom glanced in the rearview mirror before buckling her belt.

Abby shoved me. "You didn't tell her?"

"Tell me what?"

As my mom twisted to face me, I knew one thing for sure. No matter what happened to her and my dad, my life could move forward. Camp, Ethan, Juilliard. I'd embrace them all.

I pulled my sunglasses over my eyes. "I've been selected to go to composition camp next summer. In New York."

Better start composing the score. My life's symphony would need one. And, the masterpiece would be epic.

Beethoven. Bach. Mozart. Watch out for Bruchi.

Falling Flat

Reasons I like Camp-

14. Unexpected wins
15. New dreams

ABOUT THE AUTHOR

Growing up around music and dance, Jenna Brooke Carlson developed a love of the performing arts at an early age. The smells of sweaty feet and metallic spit were almost as familiar to her as the aroma of her Italian mother's cooking. Realizing she'd rather be reading books than practicing scales, she gave up playing instruments, but the love of music remained.

Jenna is an elementary dual language teacher in the Chicago suburbs. As a member of American Christian Fiction Writers and Word Weavers, she enjoys spending time with other writers and perfecting her craft. Along with writing, she's pursuing her dreams of creating a community of brave young women, who she can encourage to live out their dreams amid challenges and imperfection. Her days are busy, but she's determined she can conquer anything with a fuzzy blanket and hot cup of tea.